## *What if you fall in love with the same man again?*

That danger existed. Katerina would be a fool to deny it. An attraction was there—even if she didn't remember being married to him. There was an awareness, a chemistry. Living together would provide a fertile environment for them to fall in love again. But he loved *his* Katie. Not her.

He walked past her to the door, and she noticed how well his jeans fitted. How well he wore his green shirt. How tanned and electrifying his skin was. How very male he was.

She felt surrounded by him.

Her breath skipped as he turned around and stopped.

'You won't be sorry, Katie,' he said, his gaze sweeping over her, touching her trembling lips, the vee of her sweater and the smooth fit of her trousers. The blue of his gaze snagged hers.

'Nothing will happen that you don't want to happen.'

She wondered why that didn't reassure her.

Dear Reader,

Welcome to Silhouette Sensation®! Six new sizzling titles every month.

Marilyn Pappano and Maggie Shayne have got together and brought us an irresistible 2-in-1 volume—*Who Do You Love?*—based on hidden identities and lovers who are not what they seem. That's followed by the third book in Ruth Langan's trilogy, *The Wildes of Wyoming*—*Ace* and we're certainly hoping for more from her soon.

Marie Ferrarella returns to us once more with a spin-off from her BABY OF THE MONTH CLUB series, *The Once and Future Father*—a great summer story with a brooding, protective cop *and* a secret baby. *The Detective's Undoing* is versatile Jill Shalvis' latest and links in to a previous and a forthcoming novel about three foster sisters meeting tall, tough and handsome men.

*Who's Been Sleeping in Her Bed?* and *The Temptation of Sean MacNeill* are the offerings from the relative newcomers to the list, but I have to tell you, they are cracking books. Virginia Kantra's been writing about the sexy MacNeill brothers for a while and Sean is just as gorgeous as Patrick and Con. While strong, rugged Mitch Reeves is a husband *no* woman would want to forget!

Take a look at and enjoy them all,

The Editors

# Who's Been Sleeping in Her Bed?

## PAMELA DALTON

SILHOUETTE
SENSATION

*All the characters in this book have no existence outside the imagination
of the author, and have no relation whatsoever to anyone bearing the
same name or names. They are not even distantly inspired by any
individual known or unknown to the author, and all the incidents are
pure invention.*

*First published in Great Britain 2001
Silhouette Books, Eton House, 18-24 Paradise Road,
Richmond, Surrey TW9 1SR*

© Pamela Johnson 2000

ISBN 0 373 27090 9

*18-0601*

*Printed and bound in Spain
by Litografia Rosés S.A., Barcelona*

## *PAMELA DALTON*

believes in happily ever after. She fell in love with her husband, Mark, through the letters they exchanged while he was stationed in Fort Knox, Kentucky, and she attended college in Sioux Falls, South Dakota. When he finally flew back for their first 'official' date, he popped the question twenty-four hours later, and Pamela said yes. Married to her hero for more than twenty-five years, she cherishes her quality family time with her two adult children, Betsy and Peter.

To Betsy and Peter, with all my love

I wish to extend special thanks to:
Dennis Kragness, for generously sharing his wealth of breeding knowledge.
And also to:
my mum and my sister Janis,
Peggy Hendricks, and Mary and Julia Kragness,
for filling in the bits and pieces,

and finally to Jodi, Lori and Chris, for being my backbone and support.

# *Prologue*

Tucking his knees close to his chin to keep his body from shaking too much, Jacob stared longingly at the top of the stairs.

The police lady couldn't see him hiding behind the battered trash can at the bottom of the steps. But he just knew she would when the time was right.

She spoke to another officer as they came down the steps. Next to the big man she looked small, but the police lady stood tall and proud in Jacob's eyes.

She had a soothing, soft voice, a quick smile and deep sea-green eyes. At least Jacob assumed they were the color of the sea. He'd never been outside the state of Wisconsin, but he'd looked at lots of picture books at the Bakerstown Public Library. And her eyes looked exactly like the ocean. That was the first thing he'd noticed about her when they'd come to take away his mama. The lady officer had been nice. She hadn't called him a baby, like others had. Or ignored him. She'd been kind, bending so she was eye-to-eye with him, asking his name in that soft mama-like voice. She hadn't even gotten mad when he couldn't keep all of his tears inside, or when one had dropped onto his shirtfront. She'd put her hand out and touched his cheek and said, "That's okay, honey. We'll take care of you."

She'd called him *honey*.

That's how he knew he could talk to her. His mama had called him honey, too.

Jacob waited patiently for the police lady. She wore regular clothes like his mama had. And she smelled pretty. His mama had smelled good, too. He missed his mama. A lot.

There wasn't anyone he could talk to now. No one seemed to understand the big hurt inside him. They just patted him on the head and said dumb things like it was too bad his mother had died. No one wanted to hear what he had to say.

*She* would listen and understand.

Like she had before.

"Katie, who's the perp you logged in?" asked the man next to her. He didn't wear a uniform, either, but he had a big policeman's voice that hurt Jacob's ears.

Jacob saw the Katie-lady stop and turn back to the big man. "He's been fingered by a witness in the Clark case," she said. "We're running him through a lineup this afternoon."

"You got a witness?"

"A crackhead," she said, her nose wrinkling in a funny way.

Jacob didn't know what a crackhead was, but he figured it wasn't anything good when he heard the other officer snort and say, "You might as well chuck his bracelets now and save yourself some paperwork. He's got one foot out the door already.''

Katie-lady winked. ''Not if I get him to cop a plea.''

''You going to use your sassy charm?''

Jacob liked her quick laugh as she flipped a salute with her hand and skipped down a few more steps toward him.

Jacob braced himself for the moment he'd have to leave his place and face her. He was determined to be brave.

He took a big breath.

He started to move forward, but he froze as two other police officers came up behind Katie-lady with a man wearing handcuffs. But it was the fourth man—directly behind them—that made Jacob cringe.

He had seen that man before. Only once, but it had been long enough for Jacob to know this was a scary man who did mean things.

Suddenly commotion broke out at the top of the stairs as the handcuffed prisoner broke free from the two officers. The prisoner raced straight down the steps. One officer lunged at him, but missed.

Fear brought Jacob to his feet to warn his police lady.

She spun around, but stopped short the instant her gaze met Jacob's frozen stare. He tried to speak, but no words came out.

Her green eyes widened in alarm. ''What—''

Then it happened.

There was no time for Jacob to warn her, even if he'd been able to speak.

The man ran directly into her.

Caught off balance, she pitched forward. Her arms flung backward, clutching for a hold. Instead she found air.

Someone yelled.

Someone screamed.

But the little boy didn't hear anything, except the crack of Katie-lady's head hitting the cold cement floor.

Oh, no, not Katie-lady, too! Scooting back into his tight corner, Jacob shrank against the wall to make himself invisible again. His shoulders shook, silent tears sliding down his face.

Who would help him now that both Mama and Katie-lady were dead?

# *Chapter 1*

Katerina took another stab at opening her eyes. She braved the unrelenting brightness around her before a searing pain shot through her head.

Her world wavered.

Perhaps she should sink back into oblivion where the soothing shadows comforted and kept the real world at bay.

Curiosity, plus a very dry mouth, proved stronger. Katerina struggled harder to raise her gritty, uncooperative lids. She achieved a squint and saw…spots.

Panic broadsided her. *Oh, my God, am I blind?*

No, she couldn't be.

She shifted her head slightly, away from the unabashed light. Shapes took form. Disjointed at first, but they gave her hope.

The tension in her backbone eased a bit. She'd probably been in a deep sleep. That had to be it. Her mother always complained she didn't get enough rest and ran on just a breath of air.

Katerina waited a few seconds and blinked, trying to shoo the dark blemishes away. If she was patient, her eyes would adjust. Waiting had never been her long suit.

Training her gaze at the bland ceiling for several minutes, Katerina ordered herself to stay calm and to rely on her other senses to fill in the details.

A sterile antiseptic smell teased her nostrils. She wrinkled her nose.

Was she in a hospital bed?

She had no memory of arriving at the hospital.

Numbness stole over her. Slowly she shifted her gradually clearing gaze and scanned the room. Yes, this was definitely a hospital room. Everything seemed typical of that type of institution, until her gaze landed on a strange man.

She frowned.

Why was a stranger sleeping upright in a chair just a few feet away from her bed?

He appeared to be thirtyish, give or take a few years. A navy-blue T-shirt molded the muscular frame, hugging the well-developed biceps of his crisscrossed arms. His blue jeans, looking as if they'd been through countless machine washings, encased his long legs and accented the power of his thighs.

Even with his eyes closed and his head dipping forward to rest on his chest, his rugged appearance made her think of wide-open spaces and wild beasts needing to be tamed.

He clearly didn't fit the room, or the room him. Yet his mussed brown hair and two-day growth of whiskers indicated he'd been there quite a while. The pale green walls of the room had drunk the vitality and energy from him, leaving a grim-lined exhaustion. She was fairly certain she'd never seen him before in her life. A woman would remember a man such as him.

So why was he here? More importantly, why was she?

Katerina frowned and tried to think. The black spots in front of her eyes faded into the background, leaving a large vacuum inside her muddled head. That, too, was a mystery. She usually bounded awake, instantly alert and ready to tackle the day.

She could ask the man dozing at the foot of her bed the questions bombarding her. But for some reason, she felt reluctant to draw attention to her wakefulness.

The door suddenly whooshed open. A nurse, clad in a cloud-white pantsuit, breezed into the room. Her eyes connected immediately with Katerina's, widening with pleasure.

"Well, well, look who's decided to rejoin the human race." The nurse rustled up against the bed and reached for Katerina's wrist to expertly find the pulse. "I was beginning to worry you were planning to sleep away the next ten years. How are you feeling?"

Katerina's thick tongue felt mired in molasses. "I don't know," she managed to say. Her voice sounded husky and untried to her own ears.

"Katie?"

Katerina turned, wincing at the sudden movement.

As the wooziness receded, she frowned at the strange man who had been sleeping so soundly moments earlier and was now pressed against the bed. Male heat and caged energy surrounded her, eclipsing the antiseptic hospital atmosphere.

She wrinkled her nose. His familiarity made her uneasy, and she preferred being called Katerina.

Before Katerina could correct him, the nurse released

her wrist. "Let me call Dr. Norton. He wanted to know as soon as you regained consciousness."

Katerina couldn't work her mouth fast enough to stop the nurse from exiting the room, leaving her with the unfamiliar man who had disturbing glacial-blue eyes.

His hand covered hers possessively, interlocking her chilled fingers with vibrant warmth. "Welcome back to the real world, sweetheart. You gave me quite a scare."

*Sweetheart?* The intimacy of his grip caused warm awareness to swirl through her nerve endings. She tried to pull her hand free of his, but he either didn't notice or refused to release her.

"How are you feeling?" he asked.

"Fine," she lied. She attempted to raise her head, but a wave of dizziness torpedoed her attempt.

"Hey, take it easy." He pressed her back against the pillow. "You're not ready to start doing laps yet. Let's have the doctor check you out first so you don't take another tumble."

"Tumble? I fell?" Her memory was gray. She wrinkled her nose and tried to focus her mind.

"You don't remember?" he asked gruffly.

Remember? Her head consisted of layers of fog. How could she have forgotten a fall that had landed her in the hospital?

"Did I fall at my mother's house?" she managed to ask despite the raw hoarseness in her voice.

"No, you—"

He was interrupted by the door opening again. A man wearing a white doctor's coat and sporting a salt-and-pepper crew cut and an outlandish corn-colored bow tie preceded the nurse into the room. Despite his comical appearance, sober intelligence lurked in his faded hazel eyes.

''It's about time you decided to rejoin us, young woman.'' He beamed as if he were a proud parent.

The doctor was no more familiar to her than the other man, but she didn't feel the same discomforting vibrations she did with the man with blue eyes. Breathing a little easier, she asked, ''Do I know you?''

The doctor chuckled. ''I don't suppose you do. You've been too busy playing Rip Van Winkle and missed the introductions. My name is Dr. Norton. I'm your neurologist. This is Mary. She's one of your nurses.''

Norton? Neurologist? Mary? The names and faces were alien, as if she'd awakened on another planet. She wasn't sure what he meant by ''playing Rip Van Winkle,'' either. Her fingers found the soft edge of the blanket and hung on tight. ''I went on vacation?''

Dr. Norton fished a pen-size flashlight from his pocket and then shone it into her eyes. ''Figure of speech, my dear. How's the head?''

She flinched as the light triggered a zap of pain again. ''Stuffed with cotton balls.''

''Any dizziness?''

''Not much.'' Her mouth moved stiffly, as if working on a rusty hinge. She noticed Mr. Blue Eyes hadn't gone too far away, but was listening closely.

Dr. Norton consulted her chart. ''Do you know your name?''

It wasn't readily available. She had to dig deep into the dark well inside her mind. ''Katerina Jolene Carson.''

Mr. Blue Eyes crowded her again. ''What about the rest of it?''

She sank deeper into the pillow, which wasn't easy since there was no place to escape to. ''Rest of what?''

The doctor cleared his throat noisily and gave Blue

Eyes a warning look. Katerina didn't understand what the look meant, but was relieved it silenced the other man.

"Do you know what year it is?" Dr. Norton asked.

She licked her lips and tried to think. The strange man's intensity made it nearly impossible to concentrate. What year was it? She searched the depths from where she'd plucked her name.

She took a guess. "Nineteen ninety-four?"

Her haphazard pronouncement was greeted by a grunt from the doctor.

Mr. Blue Eyes squeezed her hand. "Katie, it's the year 2000," he said, giving her a coaxing smile. "Remember?"

Katerina felt off balance, in danger of falling off a tightrope with no safety net beneath her. Her heartbeat thundered inside her chest. What year it was didn't seem nearly as interesting as his devilish grin. It had the power to seduce and charm a woman out of more than she wanted to give.

She made a superhuman effort to turn away from the grin and refocus on the doctor. "Is the date important?" she asked.

"Of course not." The doctor didn't reveal his thoughts as he jotted something on the chart. "Most of the time, I don't remember what year it is, either. I feel younger that way." He winked at her. "Do you remember your parents' names?"

"Ginny and Frank." She hesitated. "My father is dead." His death still produced a tightness in her throat.

He nodded. "What about your birthdate?"

"April tenth."

"How about the day you and Mitch got married?"

"I'm not married." Her forehead puckered. "Who's Mitch?"

Mr. Blue Eyes tightened his hold on her icy fingers. "Sweetheart, I'm Mitch. We've been married almost three years."

Shock electrified Katerina.

She dislodged her hand from his touch and slid deep under the sheets. "I don't even know you."

"Sweetheart—"

"Don't call me that. I'm not your sweetheart or anyone else's, Mr. Mitch!"

"It's just Mitch."

Suddenly she felt dreadfully tired. A tear slid down her face. She was too drained to care or to stop the Mitch person from wiping it gently away.

Dr. Norton handed his chart to the nurse before giving Katerina a kindly pat. "I think it would be a good idea for you to get some rest, dear. You've had enough surprises for one day. Things are bound to be confusing for a while but everything will be clearer soon." He inclined his head toward the hall. "Mitch, why don't you join me in my office for a few minutes?"

Katie sensed the Mitch person's reluctance to follow the doctor.

He touched her shoulder. "Katie, I'll be back later. Okay?"

Her throat filled with suppressed emotion. A pounding tormented her head. Her energy level was depleted. But she fought the healing that darkness and sleep would bring. She'd lost six years the last time she closed her eyes. She couldn't afford to lose six more.

As Mitch's hand lifted from her shoulder, she turned and grabbed it to stop him.

"Don't go. Please tell me what happened."

If he was surprised by her sudden desire to keep him by her side, it was no more than she.

Nothing about the Mitch person was familiar, but he seemed strong and steady.

Right now she needed his strength in a desperate way. He appeared to be the only one who could fill in the blanks.

She tightened her fingers around his, feeling the calloused roughness of his palm. "I don't understand what's happened," she whispered.

The Mitch person frowned, as if unsure what he should or should not say.

"Tell me how I got here. Please," she pleaded.

"You should rest."

"I can't until I know."

His blue eyes seemed to peer into her soul, looking for something. She wished she knew what it was.

"Mr. Reeves?" The nurse poked her head into the room. "Dr. Norton wanted to know if you were coming."

He looked up. "I'll be there in fifteen minutes."

The door closed.

Suddenly, Katerina found herself alone with a man who professed to be married to her.

She released his hand as if it were a hot potato. She caught the edge of the bedsheet and tugged it to her chin, knowing it was unreasonable to assume the thin covering could protect her from the unknown. Yet she needed something.

Mitch hooked his foot on a chair and dragged it forward. The chair creaked as he sat. "Where do you want me to start? Our meeting? The wedding?"

She shook her head. "Just tell me about the accident." That was all she could handle right now.

He leaned forward, rubbing his palms across his face

as if he needed to fortify himself. "You went to work at the police department on a Friday morning."

"I was a police officer?"

"You've been a detective for nearly two years."

Katerina swallowed and turned away so he couldn't see her despair. "Go on."

"From what I've been told, it was pretty much of a normal day until around noon." He paused. Pain flickered across the gravity of his features.

"What happened then?"

"You were getting ready to leave the building to meet me for lunch. On the way out you stopped to talk to one of the other police officers.

"As you started down the steps, a couple of uniforms lost control of a prisoner. The guy made a break for it. He knocked you from behind, and you landed on the cement floor and were knocked unconscious."

The rawness in Mitch's tone told of his anguish.

She licked her dried lips. "Was I out for long?"

"Dr. Norton performed surgery to relieve pressure on your brain. You were unconscious for almost two weeks."

Katerina let go of her grip on the bedding to reach up and touch her head. For the first time she discovered the bandages covering the left side. She tried to find a movie reel hidden inside the recesses of her mind that would play back any footage of the story he told.

She could vaguely recall her twenty-third birthday party, her father's funeral and registering for classes at the junior college. But other than those few fragments, she didn't remember much else.

Suddenly she was drained and hurting. She no longer had the strength left to fight the darkness that beckoned.

And she no longer wanted to. Sleep seemed more familiar and safe than the real world.

Her eyelids weighted down. Sleep was only half a beat away. She knew she couldn't hold off much longer.

"Mr. Mitch?" Her voice sounded far, far away.

"It's Mitch. Just Mitch."

"Don't leave me."

"Never." He gently reclaimed her hand and wove his fingers through hers.

His presence comforted her in an odd way. She didn't know why she believed he'd stay, but she did.

Katerina's eyes cracked open one final time. "I'm not married to you. A woman wouldn't forget she had a husband."

Her last act of defiance zapped her remaining energy. She fell asleep with her hand still entwined in his.

His wife couldn't see the pain cross Mitch's face or feel the bleak coldness that settled in his heart.

*Ah, Katie, my love. Leave you?*

His life began and ended with her. How could she not know? Not remember?

He leaned over and brushed a kiss against her forehead, inhaling her sweet scent.

Lifting his head, he stared at her face, her features so familiar and precious, her hand so comfortable and perfect within his own. Beneath that thin blanket were a pair of long, elegant legs that could wrap around a man's waist and hold him tight. Just a few weeks ago, her lips had curled in mischief and passion. An odd combination for sure, but all Katie.

The burn simmering inside him reminded him of the combustible attraction between them. It had been instantaneous and devastating from the first time they'd met.

The woman in front of him still had the power to seduce and arouse him inside this cell of a room. How could he still have her and have lost her at the same time?

Mitch couldn't pull his gaze away from Katie as she slept. The exhaustion had bleached her too pale features.

The few freckles that paraded across her pert nose were the only color on her face. Her shoulder-length, silky, reddish-brown hair framed her face, along with the white bandage.

Her lips, which tilted naturally upward, were drawn and lifeless. Only the normalcy of her rhythmic breathing and the hold she had on his hand told him she was sleeping and not in another coma. For that he was grateful.

Would he ever be able to relax and let her out of his sight again?

He'd come so close to losing her. The tortured memory gave birth to icy gooseflesh racing across his skin. Over the past few weeks he'd watched every breath she took, matching his with hers. He'd done everything but will her back to life from the moment he'd learned of her accident. He'd survived the purgatory of endless nights and days while she lay unconscious in the hospital. Had this happened because of his own pigheadedness those weeks before the accident?

The guilt gnawed at him, making him hurt as nothing ever had.

Katie had defined happiness and light from the moment he'd first seen her winsome smile.

He hadn't fallen in love. He'd taken a nose-dive into love and never regretted a moment of it.

If he'd worried about any danger surrounding Katie's job, he would have been more concerned about her being hurt in a high-speed chase or caught in gunfire.

Katie had always assured him she was careful. Bakerstown, Wisconsin, wasn't a high-crime city. The few problems that drifted northward from Chicago were greeted by a well-funded police force. When she'd made detective two years ago, he'd been more than a little relieved she was off the streets. They'd celebrated. He could still remember that night.

*God, Katie!* How could you forget *us?*

He wouldn't accept it.

Mitch tightened his fingers around hers. He couldn't resist the urge to touch her, coaxing a wayward strand of hair away from the corner of her mouth. She frowned a little in her sleep, but didn't protest. Her hand suddenly pulled out of his and tucked under her chin. The innocence of her position was at distinct odds with the calamity of her circumstances.

Was it only a short time ago she had reached for him in her sleep and curled into his arms? It seemed like an eternity. He planted another kiss on the top of her head, his lips savoring the silk and texture of her skin.

She still smelled like his Katie.

*Katie will remember. When you get her home, she'll remember.*

He had to believe that.

## *Chapter 2*

Katerina's taste buds no longer discerned flavors. Her nose couldn't detect smells of any strength or variety. And most frustrating of all, she still didn't remember her husband, Katerina brooded eight weeks later. She stared unseeingly out the window of her room at the convalescent home and faced the hard truths about her life as she now knew them. Six years were gone from her memory. She'd been able to learn a lot over the past two months of intensive therapy and rehabilitation, but she still knew nothing about her marriage to Mitch Reeves. The chances were she never would.

The late March wind rattled the windows, and her ears caught the sound of the familiar footsteps coming down the hallway. She stiffened. She recognized Mitch's tread moving closer to her: strong, clipped and confident. She no longer thought of him as Mr. Mitch or that Mitch person. But she had trouble treating him as she did the orderlies, the members of the police department who stopped by to see her quite frequently, or the doctors. She couldn't relax around Mitch.

She wasn't scared of him. He'd done nothing to make her fear him. If anything, he'd been exceptionally patient and tender with her, despite his strong arms and powerful appearance. But there were subtle undercurrents between them. With no other person did she feel this crazy attraction. Without even looking at him, she could feel his moods as they shifted.

Her hyperawareness probably generated from the fact he considered himself her husband.

Just the thought made her go cold and then hot. Surely it must be some other woman who had gone through a wedding ceremony with a man she didn't recall even meeting.

Katerina let out a long sigh. The howl of nature on the other side of the windowpane echoed back at her. She wished she could remember just one small detail so the puzzle pieces in her mind would come together and make sense. She'd been given scraps from people here and there.

She now knew that after her graduation from the police academy, her mother, Ginny, had sold their home and moved to Arizona. A year ago Ginny had met a man named Duane, whom she was intending to marry. Katerina had spoken to Duane several times on the phone. He'd seemed pleasant, and Katerina was happy for her mother. Ginny had been very lonely since Katerina's father's death.

Ginny was unable to come visit due to high blood pressure following a minor stroke. Her mother assured Katerina it was nothing serious, merely a sign of old age. As soon as her bossy doctor allowed her to fly, her mother promised she and Duane would come to see her.

Katerina couldn't help but wish Ginny still lived in Bakerstown. There were questions she wanted to ask that were hard to address long distance. Her mother had adamantly confirmed that Katerina was indeed married to one Mitchell Peter Reeves. And very happily, too.

Ginny's assurances had done little to alleviate Katerina's growing nervousness.

As Mitch's footsteps grew louder and came abreast of the door, Katerina rubbed her arms and tried to brace herself for whatever lay ahead. A face-off with Mitch contained too many uncertainties, and she still knew so little about him. Until now, she'd been able to postpone dealing with him.

The minute Mitch came into the room, she knew she wasn't prepared.

Katerina felt perspiration break out across her body. She tried not to show how unsettled he made her as his see-all gaze swept her frame from head to toe, taking in her black silk sweater and fitted slacks.

His vivid blue eyes, which could be cold or warm depending on his mood, found and trapped hers. "You look terrific," he said, his deep drawl eliciting a tremor down her backbone. His gaze gleamed with undisguised male appreciation.

"Thank you." She hoped he didn't notice her breathlessness. The space between them shrank to a shallow level of intimacy, making her distinctly uncomfortable. He oozed a confident sexuality that dominated the entire room and made her much too conscious of being a woman.

She struggled to resist the pull and to curb her weird fantasies. She had to be strong and firm.

Trying to not show her nervousness, she fingered the

plush knit of the sweater she wore. "It feels strange to have on real clothes for a change."

He gave her a slow grin, the corners tipping upward to meet a brief flash of dimples. "You'll get used to them. We all do. Unfortunately."

The hint of sensual teasing made her cheeks warm. It was hard to think when he was this close.

Mitch gestured at the full piece of luggage lying on the bed. It was filled with all the gifts she'd received and the few clothes he'd brought her over the past few weeks. "Since you've got everything packed, why don't we get you checked out? It's a twenty-minute drive to the farm."

She blocked him by stepping protectively in front of her suitcase. "No. I can't."

"You can't?" His grin collapsed into a frown. He scanned the small room and then looked back at her, his expression carefully blank. "Everything looks ready."

"It's not. I mean, I'm not." She took a deep breath and tried to calm her nerves. "I'm sorry. I'm not explaining this very well, am I?"

She saw the indecision on his face, but fortunately he didn't reach for the suitcase again.

In an effort to ignore the waves of heat that seemed to roll from his lean, athletic frame and skew her thinking process, she moved away from his proximity. Since she'd awakened from the coma, her mind didn't always flow along normal channels. She had to concentrate hard and formulate her words with care.

Even though she'd established some distance between them, her retreat didn't help much. She still felt fuzzy. She had no choice but to push the words out and hope he'd understand. "I want you to know how much I appreciate everything you've done for me, Mitch. You've been so kind and—"

He cut her off. "I haven't done anything any other husband wouldn't do."

She lifted her chin. "That's just the point. I don't remember marrying you. How can I be a wife to a man I don't know?"

Tension crackled through the air.

"I know you don't remember me, Katie, or anything about the life we shared, but I've got a marriage license that proves we are married," he responded with low, measured words.

She lifted her hand to her temple where she had combed over her hair to cover the scar left by the surgery and began to worry the place where the bandages had been. "I don't see how this can work. I've changed. I'm not the woman you married, and I don't have a clue how to be her."

For a moment Mitch didn't say anything.

Silence crawled between them, lengthening until Katerina thought she'd scream.

Finally he asked, "What do you want?"

"I don't want to hurt you any more than you've already been hurt." There was no easy way to cushion the reality. "But I can't be your Katie. I want a divorce," she blurted.

Mitch made a supreme effort to keep his alarm from showing, even though his heart was galloping at a record pace from sheer fear.

He shouldn't be surprised by her blunt statement, the reasoning side of his brain said. Katie had been temperamental since the head injury. But the doctor had assured him her outbursts weren't unusual and didn't always indicate a true state of mind.

"I know you're scared, and you think you don't know me," he said carefully. "But you don't have to worry.

I'll be a good husband. It'll take time for us to get to
know—''

She thrust her hands out to stop him. ''I know you're
a good man, and I know you loved your wife. But I'm
not her. I'm not the woman you married. The doctor has
made it clear he doesn't expect my memory to return.
Ever. Time won't change that. What you believe we once
had is gone.''

Mitch's mouth went dry. He tried to find the right
words, but it was damn hard. Talking had never been his
strong point. Katie had teased him about that often
enough. He was tempted to give in to the caveman urge
to toss his woman over his shoulder and carry her out
the door. He placed steadying hands on her shoulders
instead, hoping she'd feel the reassurance he was trying
to offer.

''Katie, honey, I know how hard this is for you,
but—''

''Please don't call me that.'' She slipped out of his
hold. ''I'm Katerina.''

In any other situation he might have smiled at her protest. It was ironic how much she sounded like the old
Katie when she got her back up.

He, of course, was the only one to see that.

He chose a different tact. ''It doesn't matter what you
don't remember. It's the future that counts.''

She shook her head almost violently. ''If I've learned
anything over the past two months, it's that everything
matters,'' Katie said. ''I've gone through endless hours
of therapy, relearning things that most people only have
to master once in a lifetime. I've had to accept that each
action has its own challenges, demands and accountabil-
ity.''

Before he could argue, she wrapped her arms around

herself and hugged tight. "I can't afford to ignore what doesn't feel right," she finished with quiet determination.

Mitch swallowed hard. The pain inside him was sharp and relentless. What could he say?

She touched the edge of the bed and nervously pleated the covers with her long, elegant fingers. "I wish I could change everything that has happened and give you back the woman you married," she said in a soft, wistful tone. "But wishing isn't reality. The woman you married no longer exists."

Mitch jammed his hands into his pockets. "So we'll start over."

She shook her head and gave a humorless laugh. "I barely know who I am. It's going to be hard enough trying to figure out what I want to do with my life without worrying about what you need and expect from me, too."

Mitch found himself frozen in place. He hated feeling helpless. It wasn't a condition he could accept easily. He'd always found a way to make life work for him. Yet this situation was beyond him.

Katie or Katerina. How could he separate one from the other? The woman standing in front of him was his wife. A knock on the head couldn't change that, no matter what she called herself.

What would Katie do if he pulled her into his arms and tried to rekindle the exquisite passion that had always burned between them? It had been a hundred twenty-two days, three hours and sixteen minutes since he'd made love to her the last time.

He hurt in every pore of his body.

She didn't even realize the significance of the clothes he brought her to wear. He'd given her the black silk sweater and black denim jeans last Christmas. The way she looked today—her shoulder-length hair gathered and

anchored at the back of her head with a red ribbon, showing off the creamy arch of her throat—almost taunted him
with the memories of the day she'd opened his gift. She'd
stripped down to her panties and donned the outfit. Of
course, she hadn't worn the new clothes long. But it had
been long enough—long enough for him to remember.

Raw need tormented him as his mind revisited the past
and those special moments between them.

He couldn't force his gaze away from the tender curve
below her chin or forget the taste and texture of her skin.
She had always been so sensitive at the base of her neck.
They had created a game between them.

*My neck is off limits,* she'd argue.

*No, every part of you belongs to me,* he'd insist.

The repartee inevitably led to foreplay. And the foreplay fueled hot, steamy sex.

Mitch remembered everything too well, too completely. A tug originating from the lower part of his body
became urgent and needy.

Even when times had been tough between them, they'd
always had the passion.

Katie didn't remember any part of that, either.

His gaze lifted to her face, taking in her green eyes,
now clear and focused. She'd regained the use of her fine
motor skills through extensive therapy. The pallor of her
skin had faded, and her natural creamy tone had returned.
She almost looked like the old Katie.

Almost. Mitch struggled to tamp down his desire. This
was neither the time nor the place.

He should have expected Katie's fears. Unfortunately
he'd never been good at sorting through emotional issues.
His deficiency had almost destroyed their marriage before. He refused to screw up again.

"I married you for better or worse," he said quietly.

"Just because we've hit a snag doesn't mean I'm throwing in the towel."

Her expression contained a sliver of sadness. "This is worse than the worst."

"No, it's not," he replied, despite the tight hold he exerted on his jaw. "The worst was when I thought I'd lose you forever and I'd never see the light in your eyes or hear you whisper my name."

She released the hold she had on her arms and curled her fingers into fists. "I don't remember making vows to you," she said. "They might have meaning to you, but they don't mean anything to me."

Suddenly with no warning, tears started to roll down her face. Agitated, Katie dashed them with the backs of her hands and turned her back on him. "You married someone else. Someone who doesn't exist."

"You exist."

His assurances only caused the tears to flow faster. "Look at me." She swung back toward him, her color high and blotchy. "Is this how your Katie was? Did she cry when she wanted to be mad? Or laugh when she wanted to cry?"

Mitch knew she hated the lack of control she had over her emotions since the accident. Her head injury made her prone to bouts of irrational emotion. To him, these spurts didn't count for anything. But to downplay them would make a mockery of her feelings and everything she'd gone through.

Mitch kept his hands firmly anchored inside his pockets, even though he wanted to drag her to him and soothe away her fears. Touching her would be heaven and hell. She'd reject any attempt on his part to take away her control. She'd fought too hard to regain it.

Katie moved around the room, her hands clenching and

unclenching in agitation. "Doesn't it bother you that I
can't remember our courtship, or how we met, or what
our plans for the future were?"

Mitch swallowed hard. What could he say? That he
wasn't bleeding from the loss? That he'd been so insig-
nificant, his wife had forgotten everything they ever did?

Even though he knew better than to admit those truths,
they hurt. He couldn't deny it. He wouldn't.

She stepped in front of him. Her green eyes culled his
secrets, not allowing him to hide. "Don't tell me it
doesn't bother you that I can't remember the first time
we kissed or made love."

The back of his eyes burned. She was scraping his
soul. "I'll live with it," was the best he could do.

"Can you? I can't. I don't know what side of the bed
you sleep on. I don't know if you leave the cap off the
toothpaste or if you take sugar in your coffee." She
sucked in a sigh and looked down at her trembling hands.
"Do you know what bothers me the most?"

"What?"

"I don't know what kind of dreams you created with
her. What kind of family the two of you wanted. If you
wanted to have ten kids or three."

Each word was a blow. She didn't realize how close
she'd come to slicing him open.

Mitch could barely breathe. "What do you want me to
say? That the past didn't happen?"

"No. But the answers to these mysteries are obliga-
tions and expectations I have no way of knowing, let
alone fulfilling. My memory is gone. I can't change that.
However, I do have a choice whether or not I want to
compete with a ghost of another woman." She brushed
her fingers through her hair, worrying her scar. He noticed she did this whenever she was under stress. "Even

if your Katie had my eyes and my hair color, I'm not her. But I'll always be measured against her and come up short in comparison. I can't live with that."

"Who says you'll be measured and found short? Our marriage wasn't perfect. Far from it. We both had our faults and paid the price for them." Mitch ground the words out against his better judgment.

His admission caught her by surprise. "I thought you and your Katie were happy."

"We were happy," he said forcefully. At her look of disbelief he was forced to admit, "We had normal problems, like everyone does."

"What kind of problems?"

How could he explain? He knew eventually they'd have a discussion about the past, but he hadn't intended to tell her the grim details this soon. Not when things were so precarious between them. She had no understanding of the ties and the feelings that bound them together.

Her resistant stance told him she wasn't going to come with him if she didn't know the truth.

He had no choice. "We were separated at the time of the accident." The words tore the back of his throat.

Her glossy green eyes widened, going from shock to disbelief. "You weren't living together?"

"It was just temporary. You were house-sitting for a friend."

"For how long?"

"Three weeks and two days." He could have broken it down to the exact number of hours and minutes, too.

Katie tracked his every expression as though she didn't trust him. "Why didn't anyone mention this to me sooner?"

A wave of color edged up from under his collar. "Only a few people knew. Your mother didn't even know."

She abruptly sat on the edge of the bed. "You were getting a divorce."

"No, *we* weren't," he said with ringing denial.

"Then why were you and Katie living apart?"

He hated the way she referred to herself in the third person. "I was ready to have kids and a full-time wife, but you had just been promoted to detective and wanted to work for a couple more years. It seemed the more we talked about it, the worse we made the situation. We both needed a time-out. That's all our separation was. A time-out."

Katie's forehead creased into a frown. "And if the time-out hadn't worked, then what would have happened? Would you have ended up getting a divorce?"

Mitch inhaled sharply and then made himself relax. Nothing would be gained by getting upset. "We loved each other. Neither of us wanted to be apart. We were supposed to have dinner that night and discuss your moving home again. I'd just spoken to her—er, to you, on the phone right before the accident."

A shrewd expression, characteristic of the old Katie, took residence on her face. "You blame yourself for my—her accident."

She hit the bull's-eye. His gut hurt from the impact. Mitch needed to move. He pulled his hands free from his pockets and walked to the window. He couldn't see anything beyond the gray.

"You're smart, bright and quick. Under normal circumstances you would have sensed this guy coming down behind you."

Katie surprised him by coming to his side. She placed

cool fingers on his arm, causing his flesh to tingle with gut-wrenching need.

Since her coma, she habitually touched people. It was her way of connecting. But Mitch couldn't feel her skin against his without reacting physically. He barely contained a groan.

Her expression softened. "You can't blame yourself for an accident you never caused. It just happened. That's the nature of accidents."

The exquisite caress of her fingers almost brought him to his knees. He squeezed his eyes shut, struggling to get himself under control and to not take advantage of her closeness. Damn, he wanted to touch her. Bury his face in her thick hair. Hold her. Beg her for forgiveness.

The instant Katie's hand left his arm, he grieved the loss.

Mitch opened his eyes to discover she'd moved away from him.

"Perhaps it would be best if we did get a divorce." Her voice wasn't quite steady. "There's already been too much pain between us."

"There was more between us than that." Mitch couldn't lose her now. He searched for something that wouldn't send her out of his life forever. "We loved each other."

His unvarnished honesty pulled at Katerina's defenses. How could she make him see reason without hurting him? "The accident wasn't your fault."

"Maybe it was. Maybe it wasn't." Mitch paused for only a second. "If I am responsible, I want to be able to make it up to you. A chance is all I'm asking for. Just a chance."

Katerina turned away from him, massaging the throb at her temple, trying to think. Keeping her thoughts focused was virtually impossible. But in this case she couldn't blame her unreliable brain cells.

The problem was her strange reaction to Mitch.

He made her too aware of herself. Her heart beat in a strange way. Her skin itched. She was continually reminded of her imperfections—and that she wasn't the woman he expected her to be.

How could she live with that?

How could she be *his* wife?

She'd sensed his reluctance to tell her the truth about their marriage. That much was clear. But when he had, he'd been open and direct. He hadn't hidden his pain.

That caught her off guard, demolishing the thin shield she'd tried to keep between them.

"I'm not the woman you want, or you need."

"You won't know that unless you try."

His implacability irritated her. "You'll have expectations I won't know how to meet."

"The same holds true for you."

"How?"

He anchored his fingers through the belt loops of his jeans, not coming any closer, allowing the distance between them to provide her with a safety cushion.

"When two people marry, they think they know each other," he said. "But it takes time and familiarity for them to bond. For you…Katie and me, we still didn't know each other that well. If we had, we wouldn't have been separated."

His logic sent her mind scrambling for the illogical. "Wouldn't it be better for both of us to dissolve the marriage?"

"Better is not always the best." Mitch's intense gaze didn't cut her any slack. "How will we know what's the right thing to do if we don't try?"

The tender pads of her fingertips still tingled from the feel of his hard-muscled arm.

He was too dangerous.

He was too male.

How could she live in the same house with this man if she couldn't even think when he was in the same room?

She shook her head, desperate to keep clearheaded and in control, just this once. "I'm sorry, Mitch. I don't want to hurt you, but I can't," she said pleadingly. "I can't step into another woman's role."

For a long time, neither of them spoke.

Silence deafened the room.

Finally, Mitch's shoulders sagged in defeat. "Have you thought about where you'll go after you leave here?"

She dragged in a ragged breath. "I thought I'd ask around and see if there's an apartment nearby I can rent."

"Will the doctor let you live on your own?"

"I don't..." She shook her head. "No, he said he wouldn't." She bit her lip to keep her frustration inside. The doctor had been quite emphatic he'd release her only if someone was available to assist her for a couple of months. Physically, she was getting stronger every day. But she was still struggling with short-term memory problems. The doctor didn't want her forgetting to turn off an electric iron or something similar, even though a great part of her rehabilitation therapy had been directed toward learning the coping skills to handle these everyday situations.

"You could recuperate at the farm." Mitch made the suggestion in a low-pitched, neutral voice.

"The farm?"

"I have a cattle breeding operation on the outskirts of Bakerstown," he reminded her.

"I don't think—"

"At the farm, you wouldn't be forced to deal with the distractions of the city," he said. "I could drive you back and forth for your doctor's appointments until you're ready to handle a car again."

Katerina was tempted. She desperately wanted to leave this facility and start living a normal life.

She eyed him dubiously. "What about the other Katie?"

He frowned. "The other Katie?"

"I can't be her. I mean…I'm not her. That woman is gone."

His gaze became hooded. "I'm not asking you to be my wife."

"What would I be?"

"We could work at being friends."

She wished she could read what was behind his gaze. If she knew him better she might be able to understand his intentions.

"We'll just be friends?" She tested the word on her tongue. She had trouble picturing Mitch as just a friend. Could a woman be a friend to such a virile man?

"Friends help each other," he noted. "You can use your things that are still at the house. I'll be nearby if you need anything. Otherwise, you'll have the place to yourself."

If only she could picture his farm in her mind, she might be able to foresee what problems could arise. He told her that he raised cows. She didn't know anything about cows, but then she didn't know much about anything at this point.

She licked her lips. "What about sleeping arrangements?"

"I've got an extra bedroom. You can stay there."

''For how long?''

''Does there have to be a time limit?''

''Yes. We both need it.'' This was one thing she knew for certain.

''All right. Six months.''

Before the words left his mouth, she was shaking her head. ''A month should be long enough for me to learn to live on my own.''

''Let's make it two months. Then you won't have to make any hurried decisions. There are places to hike around the bluffs overlooking the farm. And Clancy could use someone to run him a bit. He's getting a little paunchy.''

She blinked, trying to make sense of this new topic of conversation. ''Clancy?''

''Your—I mean, the dog.''

''You have a dog?''

''He's almost two years old, but he's Katie's baby.''

She instantly sympathized with the puppy. ''I bet he misses her.''

''Yes, he does,'' he said with a husky growl.

They weren't talking about the dog anymore. The hairs on the backs of her arms suddenly stood on end as something stirred within her. Her breathing changed. Her breasts felt heavier. There was a strange surge of energy, even though they hadn't changed their positions. It was distinctly intimate. Forbiddingly sexual.

''Do you like dogs?''

His innocent question caught her unaware. She had to dissect the words and translate the question. ''Yes, I think so,'' she answered slowly.

Had she imagined that spurt of sexual tension between them? Maybe he did only want to be friends, and if the dog needed companionship, they could be company for each other. It would be less lonely for her.

She tried to weigh the consequences, but Mitch's presence made it difficult to keep her mind on track.

Being confused wasn't a foreign state to her.

Mitch also made her tongue-tied and ill at ease. She wasn't like that around other people.

She tried to tell herself it was because of the expectations Mitch was certain to have. Yet, so far, he'd never really demanded or expected anything from her. Were the worries only inside her head?

He was asking to be her friend. That sounded reasonable and safe enough. Was that possible? Could there be a friendship between them? After all, they'd shared more than that at one time, even if she couldn't remember a single incident from their marriage.

She certainly could use a friend. Someone who understood something about her past life and could give her some guidance. If Mitch was willing to forgo his role as a husband and take a different, less threatening one, he might be the answer.

Who else knew her better? Who else understood the choices and options she needed to address?

In the midst of her internal debate, Mitch walked to the window again, his hands locked behind him.

With his back to her, she was free to study him.

He seemed so alone and solitary.

She tried to see the last few months through his eyes. His loss was greater than hers. She could resent the hole in her past, but she didn't have emotions invested in each day and episode that had been erased. He did. His loss was personal.

The urge to comfort him gripped her. She longed to touch him, but restrained herself. Touching Mitch was different than when she reached for others. It was distinctly more intimate. She couldn't afford that right now.

Maybe they both had something to give one another.

They could build a relationship based on support instead of loss and expectations.

As friends, she and Mitch could give each other so much.

*But what happens if the friendship evolves to something else? What if you fall in love with this man?*

That danger existed. She'd be a fool to deny it. An attraction was there—even if she didn't remember being married to him. There was an awareness, a chemistry.

Living together would provide a fertile environment for them to fall in love.

Eyeing the man in front of her, she worried her lower lip, feeling his masculinity pull at her. He made her want and yearn for things she didn't understand and should avoid.

He loved *his* Katie. Not her.

If Katerina kept that knowledge between them, perhaps they could create a friendship.

Did she really have a choice?

Staying in the country would give her the opportunity to learn who she was. She had some hard decisions to make that had nothing to do with Mitch.

What would she do with her life? What skills did she have? What skills would she need to acquire? She didn't remember anything about her job with the police department.

Perhaps she should quit fighting Mitch's suggestion and take the option he offered. For now, at least. Two months wasn't so long.

"All right," she said, saying the words fast before she could change her mind. "I'll stay at the farm."

Mitch had seemed relaxed, but as he unlocked his fingers she saw the blood return to the whites of his knuckles. "Why don't I talk to the doctor and see how soon we can get you checked out of here," he said.

He walked past her to the door, and she noticed other things about him, as well, such as how well his jeans fit his buttocks. How well he wore his green flannel shirt. How tanned and electrifying his skin was. How very male he was.

She felt surrounded by him.

Her breath skipped as he turned around and stopped.

"You won't be sorry, Katie," he said, his gaze sweeping over her, touching her trembling lips, the vee of her sweater and the smooth fit of her pants. The blue of his gaze snagged hers. "Nothing will happen that you don't want to happen."

She wondered why that didn't reassure her.

## Chapter 3

Katerina prowled the great room, trying to get her bearings in the strange house. She could feel Mitch's eyes tracking her movements.

The house was attractive, albeit totally unfamiliar. She gazed up at a picture that hung over the fireplace.

"I like this tropical print. Have you ever been to this place?" she asked, hoping to break the unnatural silence between them.

"No, it was created from the artist's imagination." Mitch set her suitcase down in front of a narrow hallway that was located to her right. "We bought the painting on our honeymoon."

Katerina managed to hang on to her smile. Just barely. Everything in this house would have some part of another woman associated with it. She had to be prepared for that.

She left the print and sauntered to the patio door, which overlooked a river.

An inhuman howl erupted from behind her.

Startled, she spun around. "What's that?"

Mitch grimaced. "Clancy. I'd better let him in or he'll tear the place apart."

Without another word, Mitch left.

Katerina heard the outside door slam before she sank down onto the edge of the couch.

It already seemed like a hundred hours since she'd left the convalescent home.

A lonely ache unfurled deep inside her. Perhaps she'd made a mistake to agree to this type of living arrangement.

She already missed the familiarity of the staff and the room she'd lived in for the greater part of two months.

A muffled bang alerted her to Mitch's return. She'd no more straightened than a big ball of fur hurtled through the air and pounced on her.

"Oh, my!" she gasped as he planted his paws against her chest, toppling her backward. The excited dog bathed her entire face with his wet tongue. She broke into laughter, unable to withstand the dog's enthusiasm.

"Clancy, get down! I told you to behave yourself or you'd have to sit in the barn." Mitch snagged the dog's leash and pulled the squirming animal off her. "Sorry, Katie. He was ready to tear down the shed to welcome you home."

The homely dog, all golden except for dark expressive eyes and an ultrapink tongue, pawed the air and whimpered in obvious distress at not being able to reach her.

Katerina couldn't withstand such pleading. She gingerly reached out and patted the prickly fur. "That's all right. You can let him go."

Mitch didn't release the dog, but he did allow him to get close enough so Katerina could stroke him. The dog's

tail waved spasmodically from side to side with such fe-
rocity she was surprised he didn't topple off balance.

"He looks like he's smiling." She felt confident about
leaning across with both hands and scratching behind the
animal's ears.

If anything, the tail wagged even harder as the canine
strained to climb aboard her lap.

"He seems glad to see me."

"He missed you."

There was an edge to Mitch's voice she didn't want to
consider too closely, reminding her she wasn't the person
either dog or his master desired.

Her limbs felt suddenly limp, her body numb and
drained. The day, the house, the man and a dog were all
too much. She wanted to find a place to curl up and nurse
her wounds.

She pulled back her hand. The dog rested his head on
her knee and lifted a questioning eyebrow at her.

"Clancy, I think your mistress needs some rest."
Mitch reached down and tugged Katerina to her feet.
"Come on, Katie, I'll show you where you're going to
sleep."

The dog stuck close to her side as she followed Mitch
into an airy room with two big windows and a queen-
size bed. "Oh, how lovely," she couldn't help saying.

The cream-colored room contained a bright cranberry
wall hanging. A huge assortment of matching pillows
were strewn across the big brass bed.

Mitch eyed the room critically. "If there's anything
you need—such as towels, an extra blanket…"

"No, everything is perfect. I'll be fine," she assured
him.

She desperately wanted to be alone before she burst
into tears.

Mitch didn't look convinced, but he seemed to understand her need for privacy. He gave one last look around the room, as if to check for himself that everything was in order, and then he reached for Clancy's collar. "Come on, mutt, your mistress needs a nap."

The dog whined.

"He doesn't have to go," Katerina protested, missing the dog's comforting heat.

"Yes, he does. He'll pester you for attention, and you need to get some rest."

She didn't have the strength to argue with him. Besides, she knew it was better for Mitch to leave so he didn't see her all achy and vulnerable. She could feel tears starting to build at the backs of her eyes. Crying in front of him twice in one day would be more than she could stand right now, even if she could blame her head injury.

She gave the dog a half smile, scratching him once more behind the ears. "I'll play with you later. Okay, fella?"

The dog's tail moved back and forth in agreement before his master pulled him from the room.

The door closed, and Katerina found herself alone.

Part of her was relieved. The other part felt more alone than she ever wanted to be.

As soon as Mitch closed the door, Clancy plopped down with a huge sigh and sprawled out protectively. No amount of coaxing would budge the canine. Now that his mistress was finally home, the big dog seemed determined to stay close.

Mitch headed to the kitchen. He picked up the newspaper and tried to read.

The print blurred. He threw down the paper and gave up the effort. What was the use?

He was at war with himself, trying to blot out the desires and needs he still fostered, and it wasn't working.

He'd hoped against hope that coming home would trigger something for Katie. But he couldn't con himself any longer. His wife hadn't remembered anything about this place or their past. Despite the doctor's warnings about false expectations, Mitch realized he'd still harbored hope that his wife would recall something of their life together. He would have settled for a small memory of the picture or the fabric of the curtains.

Katie hadn't even remembered Clancy.

God, she'd loved that dog.

*She'd loved you, too.*

A giant knot formed in his chest.

He hurt in a place that had no cushion.

Grabbing his jacket, he strode toward the door.

The March wind chafed his face and ears as he headed toward the feedlot. At the last minute he changed his mind and veered to his left, tackling the incline of the hill behind the house with long, purposeful strides.

Beneath the large evergreen, he stopped and found his breath.

Staring at the thicket of trees covering the slope, Mitch noticed the trees hadn't yet started to bud. They would soon. He wished he had that kind of assurance. It would make things so much easier if he knew his relationship with Katie would blossom within the next couple of months.

Lowering his head, Mitch thrust his hands into his pockets and continued his walk through woods.

He stopped at the top of the knoll overlooking the river that ran along the edge of his property.

This had always been his favorite thinking place. He liked the resounding, mind-soothing quiet.

Yet today his mind and body refused to be soothed. Looking over his right shoulder to the acreage that stretched out below him, he observed the patches of melting snow adorning the rolling pasture. A herd of purebred cows grazed, their burgeoning bellies a sign of their advanced stages of pregnancy, and a sure indication this would be a good year for his balance sheet.

Turning his head, he eyed the well-groomed buildings in front of him: a large feedlot, a duo pair of towering silos and a new equipment barn. To his left was the house he and Katie had built and decorated.

He'd worked hard to build this place into a profitable enterprise. He'd been nothing more than a city kid with big dreams when he'd bought this farm. But the land had called him. He loved the rich, musty fragrance of the soil and the solid firmness of the earth beneath his instep. With the help of a few local farmers, he'd learned the basic nuts and bolts of raising cattle.

He hadn't been content to have just a mom-and-pop operation. He learned to use a computer and tap into the resources on the Internet. During the slow times of the year, he took classes at the University of Wisconsin, picking the brains of their multi-degreed professors and reading every piece of cattle breeding literature he could get his hands on. It had taken him too many sleepless nights to count, but he'd earned a profit in three years. That had been just the beginning of what was now one of the bigger cattle breeding operations in Wisconsin.

He'd created this place and earned the respect of many who'd thought he never stood a chance.

He'd been content…or so he'd thought, until Katie had walked into his life.

There had been no way to protect his heart against her.

She was the exception to every rule he'd made. He had no defenses against her. She was laughter and light. Warm but mischievous. Smart but compassionate.

He'd met her when she volunteered to coordinate the Bakerstown Police Department's Special Friends project. A program designed for kids who needed a friend to lend support, offer a guiding hand, or treat them to a day of fun, Katie immediately discovered there were more needy kids than willing adults. That hadn't stopped her. She'd started combing the community, snagging anyone she could grab.

Someone had recommended Mitch. He never knew who—probably someone who thought he spent too many Saturday nights cha-chaaing with four-legged heifers in the barn instead of two-stepping with local girls.

On a bright May morning Katie had shown up on his doorstep to ask him to be the special friend to a young juvenile who was ninety percent attitude and ten percent boy. Despite being drawn to her sexy appeal, Mitch flatly refused, claiming he didn't have time. He hadn't enjoyed his own youth; why would he want to share some smart-mouthed kid's?

In the next half hour he'd learned that the word no to Katie was just a preliminary to opening negotiations. He still wasn't sure how she'd nudged him into her pet program, but within an hour he'd found himself having to deal with a sullen-faced kid answering to the moniker ''Butch.''

When Mitch finally realized just how easily he'd been charmed out of his stance by the sexy, sassy police officer, he'd done his own bit of savvy negotiating, insisting he needed some guidance on how to deal with Butch. Before Katie could pawn him off on one of the professionals she'd conned into volunteering for the program, he'd wrangled a luncheon date. The next evening they'd gone to dinner.

Three weeks later they were engaged. Six months later they were married.

He'd believed they'd live happily together forever.

What had gone wrong?

It wasn't just Katie's accident that had them at odds with the dreams they'd planned to create....

Mitch felt the sting of the wind against his ears and pulled up his collar. Damn, it was cold. The chill in the vicinity of his heart was stronger—worse than this last blast of winter.

He had only a month or two. What would he do if Katie didn't want to stay and she left for good?

The very thought plunged ice needles down his spine.

He couldn't allow that to happen. He had to do everything in his power to make her give him a chance. To give them a chance.

Mitch gazed at the view below. Soon the muddied land would give birth to the rich green foliage of spring. Spring was the time for renewal.

Lord, if only that were true for him and Katie, too. But after today's events, he didn't have much hope. His soul was as bleak as the terrain around him. Nothing he had created with his bare hands compensated for the loss of his wife.

Life without Katie was no life at all. He didn't have a clue how to win her back.

Two hours later Katerina opened the bedroom door, feeling refreshed and in control again, to discover the golden lab waiting patiently for her. He stood, eyed her expectantly and wagged his tail with a force that would have cleared tables and then some. She reached down and gave him an awkward pat on the head.

"Nice Dog," she said, unable to recall the animal's name. He seemed grateful for her attention.

"Dog" nuzzled closer, pressing his nose against her leg and gazing up at her with adoring eyes. At least here was someone, or something, that didn't seem obsessed with their past history.

"Where's your master?" she asked, not because she was anxious to find Mitch, but because she'd endured enough surprises lately.

The dog's tail churned the air. Katerina bit back a sigh. Being the strong silent type did have its disadvantages.

She decided it didn't matter. If Mitch was gone, she was free to explore the house on her own without anyone watching her every move.

Dog acted as her tour guide, leading the way to the kitchen. On the counter, she found some grapes and a loaf of bread. Breaking off a piece of the bread, she gave it to her companion while she attacked the grapes. The fruit was as tasteless as everything else she tried. Since the accident, food had lost its flavor. She ate only to fill the emptiness in her stomach.

She pushed away the grapes and eyed the kitchen. Baskets scattered across the tops of the cupboards lent a cozy, friendly feel to the natural wood with its gleaming gold handles.

She looked at the mutt at her side. "What room do you want to show me first?"

His tail shifted into high gear.

Just then, there was a knock at the front door.

Dog charged past her, reaching it before Katerina.

She swung open the door to find a big man, who appeared to be in his mid-thirties, and a woman, who was probably just shy of thirty, standing there.

"Hi, Katie Lady. Remember us?" the man said, greeting her with a broad, toothy smile.

It took Katerina only a second to recall where she'd seen them. "You're detectives. You came to visit me a couple of times."

"Got it right the first time. I'm Rafe Henderson. Your partner." He didn't seem upset that she didn't remember his name. "This is my temporary partner, Mandy Vincent. We thought we'd stop by and check up on you. We knew you were dying for some good conversation."

The woman carried a box and wrinkled her nose. "Don't pay any attention to him. Rafe's idea of good conversation is distinctly R-rated."

Once inside, Rafe reached down and scratched the dog's ears. "Hey there, Clancy. You're looking good for a dead dog."

"Dead dog?" Katerina questioned.

"Yeah, he almost ended up being put to sleep."

Mandy snorted, giving Katerina a just-between-us-women look. "That's how you picked Rafe as a partner. You couldn't turn your back on his ugly puss after no one else would have him."

"Careful, woman, you might hurt my feelings," Rafe said without an ounce of ire.

"Fat chance."

Before Rafe could respond, Mandy thrust the box she held toward Katerina. "I brought some of your things from your desk. I didn't know if you needed them or not."

"Why don't you come in and sit down?" Katerina balanced the cumbersome package and led the way to the great room.

Rafe made himself right at home, dropping to the floor and playing with the four-legged animal. The dog raced into the other room and returned with a thick rope clenched between his teeth. Rafe grabbed one end, and the two engaged in a rigorous game of tug-of-war.

Mandy seated herself on the couch while Katerina took a place next to her.

As dog and man battled for supremacy on the floor, Katerina sifted through the stuff Mandy had given her. She found a framed photo of her and Mitch. She tucked it away, preferring to study it when she was alone.

Mandy leaned over and freed another picture. This one showed Mandy and Katie sitting on a bench in front of a big brick building.

"That's the day you and I made detective," Mandy said.

They appeared happy.

Katerina shook her head with a twinge of regret. "I'm sorry. I wish I could remember."

The other woman gave a sympathetic chuckle. "Don't be sorry. There's a lot of things I wish I could forget."

"That's because you're such a klutz, Vincent." Rafe's voice boomed from behind the wall of fur as he rolled around the floor with the dog. "If it weren't for me, you'd be lost."

"Humph!" she snorted. "The captain took you off patrol so you wouldn't shoot yourself in the leg."

"Is that the story they told you? They just didn't want you to feel bad when you learned the truth."

"And what truth would that be, oh Great One?"

"All the other yellow-bellied cowards in the department weren't experienced enough to cope with all those female problems."

Mandy glared at him. "Rafe, you're sexist."

"Me?" He widened his eyes, attempting to look hurt. "Women love me. Just ask any of them."

"I will as soon as one of their pimps comes up with bail money and gets them released."

"Dang it. They still haven't sprung them?" He hung a long face. "That shoots another Saturday night all to hell."

Katerina couldn't restrain her laughter. Their easy familiarity made her feel included. "You must have a lot of fun at work," she said.

Mandy shrugged. "We have our moments."

The lightness ended a minute later as Mitch walked into the room.

He came to an abrupt stop, looking surprised at the sight of their guests.

"Hey, Mitch," Rafe drawled.

"Rafe." Mitch shook the other man's hand and nodded at Mandy.

"What brings you out this way?"

"Mandy did some housecleaning of Katie's desk and insisted we bring it right out," Rafe drawled. "You know how women are. Always fixin' and straightenin'."

Mitch didn't look convinced.

To dispel the strained atmosphere, Katerina pulled a small camera out of the box on her lap. "Was this mine?"

"I bought it for your birthday last year," Mitch answered.

Rafe pushed the dog away and sat up. "Yeah, you had some grand plans to use it to gather evidence."

Katerina turned the small camera over. "It looks as if it was never used."

Rafe grinned. "You never took the time to read the manual or learn to use it."

"There's the instruction book." Mandy pointed to a small booklet near Katerina's hand. "The captain said he'd put you to work if you learned how to use it. We'd be glad to have you back whenever you're ready. We're shorthanded."

Rafe made a rude noise. "He's just worried about meeting the quota for minorities and women. If Katie comes back, then he won't have to hire any more train-ees." He drew out the last word, making it sound evil.

Everyone laughed, except Mitch. "Katie is supposed to be recovering. Tell Captain Loomis he'll have to look elsewhere to fill his allotments."

A tense quiet descended over the room as Mandy and Rafe exchanged looks.

Katerina cleared her throat. "I don't remember any-thing about my job."

"I was afraid of that." Rafe set aside the dog's toy. "Never mind. We'll teach you."

Clancy sighed, seeming to understand that playtime was over. He rested his nose on his forepaws, his eyes flickering to Rafe's suddenly grim expression.

It was Mandy who broke the silence. "I know our coming here seems pushy, but we've got a bit of a prob-lem."

"What kind of problem?" Katerina asked.

Rafe took a chair and sat. "A few months ago, there was a terrible car accident. A woman and her six-year-old son went off the road and hit a tree. We didn't find them until the next day, but apparently the woman died instantly."

"What about the little boy?" Katerina set aside the box. "What happened to him?"

"Physically, the kid is fine," Rafe said, his voice flat with no-nonsense professionalism. The playful edge in his earlier demeanor had completely disappeared. "But he hasn't spoken since we found him in the seat next to his mother's dead body."

"'We'? Are you saying I was there?" Katerina asked.

Rafe nodded. "We were investigating a homicide at a farmhouse down the road and stumbled onto the accident after we left the scene. The kid was bound and determined to stay with his mother until you managed to coax him out. Since then, he hasn't spoken a word."

"His vocal chords were damaged?" Mitch asked.

Mandy shook her head. "No, he just doesn't talk."

Katerina had to blink back a surge of tears. "He must be devastated by losing his mother."

Mandy nodded. "It almost breaks your heart to look into Jacob's big sad eyes. He's such a sweet little boy."

Mitch looked grim. "Has he seen a doctor or a therapist?"

Mandy nodded. "Yes, but he doesn't respond to anyone. We've been hoping that time would heal Jacob's internal wounds and he'd start to remember.

"A couple of weeks ago his grandmother called the department to report Jacob missing. She hadn't been able to find him and had been frantically searching for several hours. Before we could leave the station, Rafe discovered Jacob crouched inside the alcove of Katie's desk."

Katerina's gaze widened. "My desk? At the police station? Why?"

"Someone's letting him in but not admitting it," Rafe replied. "But since that day, whenever his grandmother isn't looking, the kid sneaks out of the house and secludes himself in that space under your desk."

"Why are you two working on this?" Mitch asked. "You're detectives. Shouldn't this be handled by social services?"

"Normally that would be the case, but we think the boy is in danger," Mandy said. "Mrs. Peterson—his grandmother—has noticed someone watching their house. Every time Jacob has slipped away and the grandmother has gone looking for him, she's witnessed a strange car parked near her house."

Katerina leaned forward. "Who is it?"

"We don't know. It could be someone completely harmless."

"Or it could be someone who's looking to get rid of a witness," Rafe added.

Katerina's mouth went dry. "Witness?"

Rafe nodded. "The person who committed the homicide Katie and I were working on might have been the same person who forced the kid and his mother off the road that night. We know more than one vehicle was involved—from the skid marks found at the accident scene."

"Isn't that a bit of a stretch?" Mitch asked.

Rafe shrugged. "We've got a homicide, a scared kid, and an unexplained accident. All those happened on the same night within a mile of each other. My gut tells me this ain't no coincidence. I don't want to end up with a dead kid because I didn't trust my gut. Dead kids are ulcer-builders."

"We consulted a child psychologist who tried to get Jacob to open up," Mandy said, "but he resisted her at every turn. He just waits by your desk."

"The kid's spooky," Rafe said. "But you feel sorry for him. He kinda gets under your skin."

"Jacob is not spooky, Rafe," Mandy objected. "He's just a lost little boy."

"Who has lost his whole world," Katerina murmured.

"I think that's exactly what he feels," Mandy said

quietly. "But we don't know how to help him. He seems to be waiting for you."

Katerina bit her lip. Suddenly everyone's eyes zeroed in on her. Even Clancy eyed her with expectation.

She'd endured endless hours of frustration since she'd awaken from her coma. But she'd never felt so helpless. "I wish I could help him, but I don't remember anything about my job or that accident."

"Katie's not responsible for this kid's mother's death," Mitch interjected.

Rafe leaned forward and met Katerina's eyes. "No, you're not responsible. But if there's anything you can do to help us…"

"What is it you'd like me to do?" Katerina asked.

Mandy placed her hand over Katerina's clenched fingers and gave them a squeeze. "We didn't come here to upset you, Katie. But we don't know where to turn, and since the boy keeps looking for you…well, we thought maybe he'd respond if he saw you."

"Do you think he'd talk to me even if I don't recognize him?" Katerina asked.

The detective shrugged. "It can't hurt."

"You're supposed to be resting, Katie," Mitch said tersely.

Her gaze found his. She saw his uneasiness.

She stood and crossed the room to where he stood and put her hand on his taut arm. "How can I rest if I know this little boy, who has already lost his mother, needs me?" she asked him.

"You don't know him. You might not be able to help him."

"Maybe not. But I know what it's like to feel lost and alone. Maybe that's all he's looking for." She tried to be gentle. She understood Mitch was trying to protect her, but she needed to do this. "If nothing else, perhaps I can just comfort him. Everyone needs someone. I had you."

Mitch could hear the fear thundering inside his chest. He'd resented Katie's job in the past. He wanted to order her to stay home, to keep away from that damn department. He didn't want to lose her to her job again. He had only a very short time to convince her to stay. Yet, what choice did he have? He could lose her either way.

His gaze locked with Katie's. In the mirrored green pools, he saw her plea for understanding. His denial died in the back of his throat.

This part of her hadn't changed. She had always had a damn soft spot for needy kids. He wished he could take some pleasure in that knowledge.

Rafe cleared his throat, disrupting the silence. "We're not expecting anything. There's a good chance the kid won't talk or have seen anyone at all. But if the person who forced them off the road knows something about that murder, we could use a break. There's a cold-blooded killer out there. We don't know if or when he'll strike again. That kid is our only possible clue right now."

The dog sighed heavily into his paws.

Mitch ignored everyone else in the room and stared deep into Katie's eyes. He saw her determination, but he saw something else, as well. She was asking for his approval. That surprised him. Katie had never asked for his approval before.

"All right," he said gruffly, "Katie has an appointment on Thursday at the doctor's. We can stop by the department if she's feeling up to it."

The room seemed to breathe again.

Rafe and Mandy stood and moved to the door.

Behind their backs, Katie flashed Mitch a smile of gratitude. Mitch made a valiant effort to match it, even though his insides were twisted in knots.

By agreeing to this, what had he really agreed to?

He didn't know.

## Chapter 4

After the detectives left, Katie moved restlessly around the room. "Working for the police department must be a rewarding and intriguing job," she said. "Did I like it?"

That was the last thing Mitch wanted to talk about. Her expectant expression prodded him to admit the truth. "You seemed to like your job and your co-workers. You lived with Mandy before we were married."

"I did?" Her eyebrows drew together as if she were trying to comb through her archive of limited memories. "I've forgotten so much. How will they help that little boy?"

"They'll manage." Mitch could see the wheels turning in her head.

He didn't like the helplessness he felt. How could he compete with the glamour of police work?

He reached for his jacket. "I've got some work to do

in my office. Do you need anything?'' he asked, almost
flinching at how stilted he sounded.

''No, I'll be fine,'' she replied.

He gave her strained features a long look, but he didn't
argue with her weak pronouncement. He had to get out
of here. At some time they'd have to talk about how they
were going to live together over the next two months.

Now wasn't the time.

Katerina sank into the smooth cushions of the leather-
upholstered couch after she heard Mitch leave. She stared
at the dog.

''We're the only ones without something to do,'' she
said to Dog. She'd forgotten his name again. Fortunately,
he didn't seem to mind.

The dog leaned forward and rested his long, quivering
nose on her lap, as if to say he understood her dilemma.

A dull ache gathered inside her temple. She could take
some of the pain medication the doctor had prescribed,
but she didn't want to rely on a drug. She'd rather face
the painful realities.

In truth, her head wasn't really the problem. There was
a big emptiness inside of her. Why had she agreed to
come here? She was out of her depth.

She had no business trying to pick up the pieces of
another woman's life.

There were serious repercussions beyond her marriage
to Mitch.

That poor little boy. How lost and alone he must feel.
He was expecting something from her, and she was certain she would only let him down.

For a moment Katerina was tempted to wallow in her
profound sense of frustration.

Her positive nature asserted itself, however. She

wouldn't be able to help anyone if she gave in to despair. That had been the creed she'd used over the past few months to get her this far. She'd refused to give in to self-pity then, and she wouldn't now.

Stiffening her backbone, Katerina looked around the room, trying to find something that would give her a plan of action.

Her gaze landed on the wedding picture sitting on the mantel.

Rising to her feet, she picked up the frame.

The photograph showcased Mitch and Katie dressed in their wedding attire. The radiant couple had eyes only for each other. A perfect pair. No one looking at this snapshot would think that they wouldn't have a happily-ever-after union.

Katerina wished she could see deeper into the picture to understand what else was there. The camera captured expressions but did little to reveal their body language, their comfort levels, or why the marriage might have frayed.

A strident ring jarred her thoughts.

She realized it was the telephone.

"Hello, dear."

Katerina recognized the sound of her mother's cheery voice on the other end of the line. "Hi, Mom."

"How are things going?"

"Great." Katerina made it a point to be deliberately vague whenever she spoke to her mother. She didn't want the older woman worrying about how ill-prepared her daughter was to deal with her perplexing life. Instead she turned the conversation around. "How are you doing? What has the doctor said?"

"The doctor is being an old fussbudget, and Duane is just as bad. He hovers over me like a worried mother."

In the background, Katerina heard a deep voice holler, "Someone needs to."

Katerina smiled. "Your Duane sounds like the perfect prescription."

"He is." There was a pause. "You don't mind, do you, dear?"

"Mind what?"

"About Duane. You haven't met him yet, but he's a dear, dear man, and he's good to me." Her mother's anxiety was clear through the phone wire.

Katerina found herself shaking her head, then realized her mother couldn't see the movement. "Mom, so long as you're happy, then I'm delighted for you. I'm sure Dad would be, too."

A sound of relief came over the phone. "Thank you, dear. I know you miss your father. I do, too. But he's been gone almost ten years. No one can replace my feelings for him."

Katerina could hear the earnestness in her parent's voice. "I know. You loved Dad."

"I still do. I always will. He was a good man. Not perfect, but good in his own way."

"Do you miss him?"

"Yes. But the real pain is gone. Now it's just an ache mingled with comfy memories that make me smile."

Katerina had a hazy recollection of her father. Medium height with a generous smile and slightly balding head, he liked to tell her stories about his job. Her recollection was a feel-good picture. Kind of happy with a little melancholy ring around the edges.

Katerina wondered if Mitch would ever think about his relationship with Katie that way.

No, there wasn't the distance of time that her mother had. Two months wasn't the same as ten years.

Katerina batted away the sense of futility and made an effort to concentrate on the present. "Do you feel the same way for Duane as you did for Dad?" she asked.

"No. Yes. I don't know," her mother said hesitantly. "It's hard to compare an old love. You have years of history that become part of the layers of your relationship. Duane and I are still getting to know each other. Plus we're bringing those past relationships with us."

Her mother giggled a bit self-consciously. "Oh, my, listen to me. I sound like a giddy schoolgirl, don't I?"

"You sound like you're in love." Katerina couldn't contain the ping of longing. At least her mother and Duane were on the same page. Mitch had the memories; Katerina didn't have anything.

"I am, and so were you and Mitch," her mother reminded her gently.

"It doesn't seem real. I can't recall anything about our lives together. I don't even remember our wedding." Her fingers reached for the scar near her ear.

"Why don't you watch your wedding video? It won't show your entire lives together, but you'll be able to observe an important part of it."

After her mother rang off, Katerina considered her mother's suggestions as she cradled the receiver. Watching the video would be proactive.

Per her mother's directions, Katerina searched through the cabinet below the television and found video footage labeled "Wedding."

Then she tried to figure out the mysterious array of buttons on the VCR. She didn't have a clue which button triggered what.

There was a knock, followed by the pealing toll of the doorbell.

Tucking the videotape under her arm, she swung open

the door to discover an outlandishly dressed stranger eyeing her expectantly. The young man, probably no more than twenty, wore a spiky haircut, several earrings dangling from his ears, and two rings through his nose.

"Hey, Katie. You're looking real cool."

"I'm not cold at all." She frowned. "The house is quite warm."

He looked confused and then smiled. "Sorry, I forgot you don't remember me, do you? I'm Butch."

"Hi, Butch." She tested the name. "Have we met?"

"I'm Mitch's little brother." He put up a hand as if to ward off what she was thinking. "Not literally, I mean. You matched us up through your kids program."

"I matched you and Mitch?" She couldn't imagine a more unusual pairing.

She leaned forward and stared at the unusual piercings adorning his body. "Do they hurt?" she asked, allowing her stream of consciousness to dictate the course of the conversation.

"Does what hurt?" He frowned. "You mean, the rings? No. I forget they're there. Do you like them?"

"Very much." Somehow they made sense on the outgoing young man.

"Mitch hates them. He says I'm going to get electrocuted or something."

Katerina grinned at the image of Mitch's disapproval.

"Is Mitch around?" the boy-man asked.

"He's out in the barn."

"Cool. I mean, I guess I'll go out and find him."

She nodded, still a bit bemused by the idea that Mitch even associated with such a colorful young man.

"Are you going to watch that?" he pointed to her hand.

She looked down at her hand and realized she was

holding the videotape. What was she going to do with it again? "I was, but I don't know how to run the machine. There are too many buttons."

"Do you want me to help you?"

"Would you?" She stepped back and allowed him to enter the room.

He whistled through his teeth as he flipped a switch and pushed a few buttons. The television came on before he slid the video into a wide-mouthed slot in the long black VCR.

The television suddenly changed from a daytime soap opera to the inside of a church. Katerina recognized Mitch's broad shoulders and serious face filling the scene.

"There you are." Butch stood and stepped back. "You can stop it by pushing this button in the middle. Okay?"

She nodded, her attention totally captivated by the scenes in front of her.

Katerina didn't hear Butch leave the house. She only heard the sights and sounds of the wedding.

Two bridesmaids wore lavender dresses. Katerina recognized one of them as the female detective.

Then Katie appeared. She was every bit as radiant on the film as she was in the photograph.

Katie watched the entire footage, and when it was over she still didn't know any more than she had before.

The dog interrupted her gloominess with a long-suffering whine.

"What's the matter, Dog?"

He rose to his four paws and trotted to the door, looking back at her with a questioning expression.

Katerina got to her feet and opened the door. A blast of chilly air filled the room. The dog didn't move.

"Do you have to go out or not?" she asked.

His wistful expression pleaded with her. Then he turned his head and pointed his furry nose at the coatrack on the opposite wall.

"You want me to go out with you?"

His tail thumped his response.

Katerina gave him a wry grin. She didn't have anything else to do. Besides, she didn't know if the dog was trained to not wander off. If he got lost, she'd be responsible. Things were hard enough without adding that to the mix.

She pulled a coat from one of the pegs and slipped it on. It fit her perfectly. She found a stocking cap on the shelf above and tugged it over her reddish-brown hair. Playing with the dog would give her something to do and help take her mind off her life.

She followed her new animal friend outside. He scampered across the yard. For a few minutes Dog raced around, chasing a dried leaf and tossing it into the air with his nose.

Katerina laughed at his exuberant play. Her fingers started to tingle from the early spring chill. She wished she'd taken the time to search for a pair of mittens. She slipped her hands deep into the warm pockets of the jacket.

To divert her thoughts from the cold, she checked out her surroundings. She hadn't paid attention to the exterior of the house and property when she'd first arrived. Now she scanned the fenced-in yard. A willow tree anchored the right corner, and a big oak sat across from it. Beyond the gate she could see a variety of outbuildings. A herd of brown cows chewed contentedly behind barbed-wire fences. The farm operation appeared to be prosperous and well-maintained.

Dog disappeared around the house. Before she could

call him back, he came racing around the other side, carrying a purple-and-black football in his mouth. He stopped in front of her and dropped his prize at her feet.

Katerina eyed the ball, then the expectant dog.

"You want me to throw it?" she asked.

The rear half of the dog's body wagged in double-time. Katerina couldn't resist such an enthusiastic appeal. She scooped up the ball and reached back to throw it.

Dog pranced next to her in anticipation. His breath fogging the air with each giant pant.

Katerina bit down on her lip, squeezed her eyes shut and heaved the ball for all she was worth.

She opened her eyes, expecting to see it sail over the fence.

Alas, the toy landed at her feet and rolled six inches.

Dog sank back on his haunches, appearing puzzled at this new twist to an old game. He looked down at the ball, then up at her.

It took all of her willpower to meet her trusting friend's imploring gaze. How could she live with the fact that she'd just disappointed a dog?

Dog didn't seem ready to quit on her, however. He waited ten seconds and pushed the ball toward her again.

Gritting her teeth, she picked up the dastardly toy. Her next effort landed an inch and a half away from the first spot. She could take heart she'd made some progress.

The dog didn't seem overly impressed. He laid down and sniffed at it. Once again, he pushed the ball back at her.

Katerina contemplated the merits of ignoring it and finding something else for them to do.

"He wants you to throw the ball."

Katerina swung around and caught sight of Mitch's

six-foot frame leaning against the white picket fence twelve feet away from her.

She couldn't keep her embarrassed blush contained below her collar. How long had he been there? The glint in his all-too-blue eyes revealed he'd been there long enough to witness her humiliation.

"I thought this might be something I could do." She gave a self-mocking laugh. "Unfortunately, I guess I can't do that well, either."

"I don't think he's complaining." Mitch picked up the ball. He handed it to her, his warm fingers brushing her chilled ones. "Clancy has a lot of patience. He's just glad to have you here."

The shocking heat of his flesh made her forget what she was doing. Against her will, Katerina's gaze collided and tangled with his. She saw his earnest determination.

Her mouth dried. The dog and his master had a lot in common.

Neither was going to let her quit.

*Is that what you want to do, Katerina? Quit?* a voice in the back of her head quizzed.

*No!* That conviction came from deep within her. No matter what, she wouldn't give in to defeat. She not only wanted to look the dog and his all-too sexy master in the eyes, she wanted to look herself in the mirror, too.

Katerina grasped the ball between both of her hands.

This time she chose a different method and pitched it underhanded. The small toy sailed a whopping five feet.

The distance was slight, but it was enough for the dog to spring into action. Mitch chuckled out loud as Clancy sprang to his feet and snatched his toy in midair before it could hit the ground. The canine bounded back to Katerina's side and offered his trophy to her.

She removed the sticky ball from his mouth and patted him on his head.

"Good dog. You are such a dear. I wish I could remember you," she said wistfully, sinking down and placing her face next to the golden animal. His tongue enthusiastically lapped her face.

Mitch plucked the ball from her fingers. "Maybe it's not important that you do."

"Do what?"

"Remember him, or any of the past."

That was the last thing she expected to hear from him. "Why isn't it important?" she asked.

The blue of Mitch's eyes darkened. "Recalling the past doesn't change what is. The dog will take whatever you want to give him. The future is what counts."

Katerina didn't know what to say. It wasn't as if she had an option; the results of her head injury were permanent. The past had no meaning to her. Fretting about it would get her nowhere.

Certainly watching the wedding video hadn't helped. She'd never understand who that Katie was, even if she wanted to.

Caught in her mental debate, she suddenly realized Mitch had said something.

"What did you say?" she asked.

"I've got some paperwork to do, so I'm heading to the barn," he said patiently.

She was instantly intrigued. She peered over his shoulder to the red barn looming sixty yards away. "You've got an office in a barn?"

"In the hayloft, to be exact."

"Can I go with you?" she asked.

She didn't want to go back into the house yet. And

she wasn't about to press her luck and disappoint the animal at her side again.

"You want to see my office?"

She tilted her head. "You sound surprised."

Mitch shrugged. "I'm just surprised you want to see it. You never seemed to be enamored with it before."

She lifted her chin and smiled widely. "That's good, then, because this will be something new for both of us. Can Dog come, too?"

Mitch answered her with a smile of his own. The crooked movement of his lips made Katerina light-headed.

"I don't think you have to worry," he responded. "That mutt is attached to your side."

He swung open the gate and allowed her to step in front of him.

True to form, the dog followed Katerina as she kept pace with Mitch. They passed a long ultra-modern shed and rounded the corner toward the barn. The imposing building was a marked contrast to the other more modern structures sprinkling the farmyard. It had old-fashioned style that echoed days of old.

"How beautiful!" Katerina said. Whatever came into her head tumbled from her mouth. "Do you have horses and chickens?"

"No chickens. I've stabled horses occasionally for city dwellers."

"Why no chickens?"

"I've never had time to take care of them. Katie didn't, either."

She frowned. "What did Katie like to do?"

He shrugged. "She was busy with her job and usually didn't spend much time out here. The farm was my turf."

"I'd say she missed a lot." She slipped past him into

the rustic interior. She tried to inhale the musty aroma but didn't have any luck. She could only imagine the scent. She looked around. "Where are the cows?"

"Out in the pasture. I use this old barn for storage and my office. There's a newer facility for the herd."

She stepped over the gutters and walked into one of the empty stalls. "Too bad for the cows."

"You really do like this, don't you?" Mitch sounded more than a little amazed. A wide grin crossed his face, lifting the corners of his mouth and evoking a matching set of dimples.

Katerina had to suck in her reaction. Damn, he was handsome. How could any woman that breathed forget a man such as him?

Don't think about it, Katerina, she ordered herself.

She returned to the main aisle. "Where's your office?"

Mitch pointed his thumb upward. "This way."

Halfway along the lower level, Mitch stopped to pull on a big rope suspended from the ceiling. A stairway unfolded to the ground. He stepped back and motioned Katerina upward. Dog stayed close at her heels as she climbed into a loft, using the rail to make sure she didn't lose her balance.

At the top, she let out an exclamation of delight. "This is perfect. You've even got bales of straw."

"I wanted to feel like I was still working on the farm, even though this office has all the modern perks."

She walked a few feet to three bales of hay that were stacked to form a bench. Sitting, she drank in the atmosphere. The wood floor had been swept clean, but maintained its rough finish. To her left was a circular desk, complete with a computer and big-screen monitor. Farm magazines were strewn across another bale. Dog saun-

tered familiarly into the loft and draped his body in front
of a big eight-foot window.

The only thing that seemed out of place was a rumpled
bed in the far corner.

"Why do you have a bed?"

He rocked back on his heels and looked a bit sheepish.
"The house was too big and lonely after your accident.
I couldn't stand being in there without you. I brought in
the old bed so I could work and make the time go faster."

"It doesn't sound very comfortable."

"I wasn't looking for comfort. I just wanted the time
to go by quickly."

"Did it go by quickly?" she asked before she could
stop herself.

"No."

The simple word and his sudden remoteness reminded
her of things she couldn't fix and had no way of understanding. Suddenly the past had rebounded, descending
between them like an unmovable gauntlet.

She attempted to redirect the conversation. "It's cozy
in here."

"I like it. This hayloft seems to bring together the old
and the new. It feels real to me."

His quiet pride told a story in and of itself. Something
inside her melted. This environment symbolized him: a
slight taming of the untamed, a mixture between the
rough and the refined, the earthy yet intimate. Qualities
that could seduce a woman into lowering her guard.

In this setting, Mitch was twice as dangerous.

She tore her gaze from his face, searching for something to break her awareness of Mitch, who was standing
too close for comfort. "I don't know if I could get any
work done out here," she said lamely.

"There's not much else to do."

"I'd want to lay on the hay and make dreams."

His grin gave way to a sexy chuckle. The deep sound resonated through the corners of the loft. "You're welcome to come out and dream anytime you'd like. You won't disturb me, and there's plenty of room."

He might not be disturbed but she knew she would be, especially with that bed in the corner.

Katerina had to remind herself she had no business thinking of Mitch in that bed. She wasn't his woman. He was a stranger. She couldn't be fantasizing about tangling in the bedsheets with him, no matter how appealing she found him.

Conscious of his eyes following her, she stood and made her way to his desk. The computer monitor broadcasted a database of mysterious numbers. "Why do you use a computer?"

"It comes in handy when I want information. I use the Internet to keep track of current production, communicating with other breeders, researching new livestock and checking out the latest breeding techniques. I can also keep up to date on what's going on in the market."

The floorboards creaked as Mitch appeared at her elbow. Katerina felt male heat wrap around her as he leaned close to punch an entry into the keyboard.

A new chart appeared on the screen, but Katerina couldn't concentrate. For all she knew it was Greek, Italian, or a combination of both. She could only think and feel the surge of warmth emanating from Mitch's solid body.

A flush rose throughout her bones.

If she didn't move, she'd probably do something stupid like push him into the straw and make her fantasies real.

What's gotten into you, Katerina? she chastised herself.

Whatever it was, she had to get rid of it.

"What did Katie do when she was here?" she asked, turning toward Mitch again. "Did she ever help you?"

"No." Mitch's mouth tightened. It was a sign she was beginning to recognize.

"Why do you do that?" she asked.

"Do what?"

"Pucker your lips in disapproval?"

"I didn't know I was."

"You did it before when the detectives were here, too."

At the mention of the detectives, a shadow descended over his features. "Did I?"

She sensed that hint of uneasiness again. She needed to understand the issues between them.

"You didn't like Katie's job, did you." Katerina didn't form a question.

His expression turned remote, and the barn didn't feel nearly as cozy. "Her job wasn't for me to like or dislike."

"Then why did it make you unhappy?"

"She was gone a lot."

"Is that why you don't like the detectives?"

"I didn't realize I was being inhospitable." His mouth turned down at the corners. "I have no feeling about the detectives one way or the other. They're good people, and they have a job to do. I wish they'd do it and not bother you with it. You are here to recuperate."

"I know that. But I keep thinking about that little boy." She placed her hand over her heart, expressing her feelings through actions as well as her emotions. "What if he won't talk to anyone else? Do you want me to just lie around and forget about it? I can't do that."

If it were possible, the temperature in the barn took a

dip. Mitch's face became uncommunicative. "I feel sorry for the kid. But that's the problem for the police. They've got enough able bodies to work on this case."

Katerina caught her lip between her teeth and gazed at his closed expression. Was he really worried about her recuperation? Or was there something more to his stoicism?

The pronounced set of his jawbone didn't look promising. She had a feeling Mitch wasn't a man a woman could mold. He'd want life on his own terms. And anyone who tried to push him in the opposite direction would have a tough row to plow.

Dog rose to his feet and meandered across the floor to her side. Her fingers automatically caressed his thick fur. He already felt familiar to her.

That was more than she could say about her comfort level with Mitch. Even though his face was now familiar, she had trouble relaxing around him.

She pushed back a twinge of desperation and strove to find some way to address the situation that most concerned her. "Part of my recuperation is to make a life for myself," she said to him. "I need to learn more than how to toss a ball to a dog. I need to find an occupation."

Mitch's forehead creased. "I'm sure I can find something for you to do around here."

"You need help feeding the cows?"

"I hire a couple of high school boys to help me, and I don't think the doctor would give permission for you to do anything too physical yet."

"What else could I do?"

"I'll think of something. Maybe you could help with the book work."

She could feel the control he was trying to exert, but she was just as strong and determined. "Sitting behind a desk would stifle me. I want to work with people. If the detectives need me, then I want to help them.''

"Is that what you want?"

She could see in his eyes that his question hid a more pertinent question.

She folded her arms across her chest. Despite her softly framed appeal, she didn't mask her determination. "Why don't you tell me what you're really afraid of so I can understand the ghost I'm facing."

Mitch looked resistant at first and then resigned. "Your job consumed your life."

"Why? Why was it so important to her?"

"Your father wanted to be a detective. He was due to be promoted when he died. His dream became your life obsession. You went to work even on the days you should have had off."

Katerina vaguely remembered bit and pieces of her father's job, but the details were blurry. She tightened her hold on her forearms. If she hadn't, she would have flung herself into Mitch's arms and tried to ease his hurt. Now was not the time to be touchy-feely.

"I'm not like that," she said flatly.

"You don't know until you get sucked into the work." He sounded raw and bitter.

His flat denouncement lit a fuse within her. She lowered her arms and glared at him. "Don't tell me what I will do just because she did it. Whatever Katie would or would not have done doesn't even matter to me. Maybe she had to prove something to her father, or to herself. I don't know what made her put her job above her marriage, or anything else. But one thing I do know is that I would never put a job before my family or another human being." She didn't try to dampen her fury.

She could no longer keep her hands to herself. She

took a step forward and jabbed a finger into his midsection to punctuate her point. ''Whatever you believe or think you know is wrong. I won't know what I want or what I'm capable of doing until I try. And I'd appreciate if you didn't assume I'll make the same choices as Katie until I've had a chance to prove who I am and what choices I'd make.''

If Mitch were any less a man, he would have found himself knocked off his feet and on his backside. Katie always had a bit of a temper, but she was blazing with fury now.

A spurt of admiration flared in his gut as he eyed the furious woman in front of him. The afternoon sun caught the rich reddish-brown hues of her hair, highlighting Katie's spirited stand. The green fire in her eyes almost made him a believer.

''I already said I'd drop you by the police department to help the little boy tomorrow,'' he reminded her.

''But you still think I'm going to turn my back on everything else once I get inside that police building, isn't that right?''

That's exactly what he feared. The doctor said Katie should be kept calm. He clamped his worry inside. There was no point in arguing about what time would prove.

Katie's gaze narrowed at his lack of response. She must have seen his denial.

This time her voice was low and firm. She met his eyes with gritty steel and steadfast determination. ''That little boy lost his mother.''

''Have you ever thought it might be better for the boy if you didn't attempt to make him believe you can fix something that can never be fixed?''

She flinched. ''Are you implying I'm leading him on because I've lost my memory?''

"No, I'm saying you can't bring back his mother. And that's what he really wants. He has a right to honest treatment. This is his reality. Life can't be neat and pretty. Sometimes it's better to be cruel than kind. It makes us tougher."

His comment had shaken her, but she stood her ground. "I don't know what kind of person would turn his or her back on a motherless little boy. Is that the kind of person you want me to be? Because if it is, you and I have nothing in common. Nothing. Unlike you, I can't just quit trying because I got hurt."

Her question stabbed Mitch directly in the heart. Katie had no way of knowing that her words were sharper than a stiletto to the ribs. The blood flowing from the wound didn't diminish as he watched her storm out of the loft.

Mitch stood motionless, listening to her footsteps fade away.

Katie's accusations surged through his head. Was he making her into someone she wasn't?

Katie had never understood his fears and his urgency to have children in the past. She didn't understand his overpowering need to cement their union.

She thought they'd had forever. They hadn't. Life had taken a turn that neither of them expected.

Now Katie accused him of not believing, but she didn't have the past to give her insight into her own soul.

Mitch hadn't begrudged his wife her dreams. He understood what it was like to want to please a parent. Lord knows, he'd tried to get his mother's attention and please her enough so she'd want to stay home with him on countless lonely school nights instead of volunteering for extra shifts at the restaurant where she worked.

But his mother had never heard or understood his needs. And when he'd married Katie, his new wife hadn't understood what it was like to not have a family. She'd lost her father, but she'd always had her mother.

No child should have to be without a mother. Ever. He, of all people, should know that.

But at the same time, Mitch thought the little boy had more than Mitch had had at that age. The kid had Katie in his corner. Mitch could easily picture all that fire directed toward protecting a child.

Mitch wanted that fire for himself. He wanted Katie to be his wife again.

But he'd lose her if he didn't allow her the freedom to make her own choices. And that scared the hell out of him.

He had to risk losing her again to win her back. He had to overcome his fears and find a new way to build a bridge between them.

He had to court Katie again.

What woman didn't like flowers?

Despite her terse discussion about the detective job with Mitch, Katerina couldn't stop thinking about the little boy who had lost his mother after she returned to the house. Questions swirled through her head. She found it safer to focus on the little boy and his situation than her strained relationship with Mitch. She didn't want to think about the pain she'd seen in his eyes. Or if she was in any way responsible.

Instead she reviewed the detectives' visit and thought of all the things she'd forgotten to ask. She spotted an address book sitting on the counter. Paging through it, she found the phone number for Mandy at the department.

Picking up the phone, she punched the numbers.

Mandy didn't seem surprised to hear Katerina's voice.

"Rafe and I had a bet about how long it would take you to contact us," the detective said.

"Who won?"

"I did." There was a definite smugness to the police detective's tone. "Rafe thought Mitch would keep you too busy to call for another day."

Katerina couldn't help but smile. If they only knew how carefully she and Mitch tiptoed around each other. "I had a couple of questions about the case you're working on."

"I thought you might."

"Who was killed in the homicide?"

"A loser, associated with the vast drug world."

Katerina rubbed her scar. "Was he an addict?"

"No. A dealer."

Since Mandy was so encouraging, Katerina kept going. "Was he ever arrested?"

"Once or twice. But nothing ever stuck."

"Stuck?"

"He was never convicted. I suspect he had a friend or two in high places. Evidence either disappeared or didn't hold up."

Katerina had trouble following the way the detective talked. "Where were the boy and his mother going? His mother wasn't an addict, was she?"

"No. They were headed to a Christmas tree farm. They had a tradition of cutting their own tree. But they never made it."

Katerina swallowed, as tears welled in her eyes.

"You're starting to get drawn into the job again, aren't you?" Mandy asked.

Katerina lowered her hand and sighed. "I don't know. I have no memories of what this job is or isn't. But I feel sorry for the child. Thanks for taking the time to answer my questions.''

''Anytime, Katie. We need you.''

Katerina hoped they weren't counting on her. She feared she was destined to disappoint everyone who was counting on her.

She was still wearing a frown when she hung up.

## Chapter 5

Dog pushed his nose into Katerina's lap. She scratched his forehead. "Life is very complicated, isn't it? How do dogs handle these problems?"

Dog didn't seem to know.

Katerina sighed. That's what she was afraid of.

There were still rooms she hadn't explored. She looked at her four-legged companion. "Why don't you take me on a tour of the house?"

The animal seemed to understand what she wanted and led her from room to room.

She found two bathrooms on the main floor. One contained a sink along with the other necessities. The second included a bathtub and full vanity. Next to that was a library with lots of books by authors she'd never heard of.

Katerina felt disoriented a few times. But Dog was a good guide. She found her way back to the bright, cheery kitchen. The bowl of purple grapes still sat on top of the center island. She popped a piece of fruit into her mouth and offered one to the dog, who finished it in one gulp.

As she reached down to pat his head, she spotted an open door just past the refrigerator.

She knew the instant she walked into the room that she'd discovered the master bedroom.

She almost turned away. But curiosity got the better of her.

It wouldn't hurt to learn a few things about the man she was living with. Perhaps she could get a better sense of what her past life had been like. Knowledge was power. That was a lesson she'd learned over and over again in therapy.

Still, she couldn't take the first step into the room until Dog walked ahead of her and turned to wait for her.

The room was as open and spacious as the rest of the house. In fact, it seemed to be a little house all on its own. The walls were cream-colored, as was the rest of the house. There was a big canopy-style bed in the center of the room, adorned with a hunter-green bedspread. She liked the bright burgundy throw pillows that complemented the colors of the room. But Katerina thought there could have been a bit more color. It was bland to her taste.

A fireplace sat in the corner, facing the bed. She flicked a nearby light switch and saw the flames shoot to life. Heat spread across the room, easing some of the spring chill.

Dog planted himself in front of the bed while she peered into the master bathroom. This room was a delight. She liked the shiny gold bath fixtures and the white whirlpool tub. A roomy shower sat off to the side, looking big enough to accommodate two people.

Several perfume bottles sat on the long ivory countertop between the two oval sinks. Curious about the kinds of scents that would attract Katie, she sniffed. She couldn't detect an iota of scent. Her nose didn't work much better than her taste buds. That was probably just as well.

Returning to the bedroom, she peeked into the closet. She did need clothes. She wanted to know what the other Katie wore.

Flipping the light switch, she was instantly taken aback by the large space that had been allotted to just plain old clothes. On the right side, men's garments hung neatly along two rows of racks. Khaki pants draped over hangers alongside an assortment of button-down and polo shirts, but the majority of hangers held men's denim shirts, in various shades of blue.

Nothing about Mitch's choice of clothing surprised her. He was a basic guy who didn't favor frills, flashy shirts or oddly colored fabrics. He wore clothes that suited the life he led. But they didn't tell her anything more than she already knew.

She reached for one of his shirts and lifted it to her face. For a moment she closed her eyes and breathed deep. She couldn't smell anything, but she could feel the essence of the man. The heat from Mitch's body seemed embedded in the soft, masculine cloth.

What would it be like to be held in Mitch's arms? To share a closet and be intimate with such a man?

A delicious excitement licked at Katerina's nerve endings. Such thoughts were tantamount to playing with fire.

She released the sleeve and thrust the shirt back onto the wire hanger.

If she was interested in knowing more, she knew she'd have to look beyond his physical appearance to learn the facets hidden inside. But was she ready to plumb those depths?

She certainly wasn't ready to address that question yet. There were too many other questions she had to explore, and one of those was to identify the differences between Katie and herself.

She turned her back on Mitch's portion of the closet and stared critically at the female attire lining the opposite side.

The first thing she noticed were the neutral, bland colors.

Disappointment hit her fast and hard.

She hadn't expected to remember the dark, conservative uniforms to her right or the mixture of dresses, pants and blouses to her left. But she'd hoped to at least feel some connection to the other Katie through their choice in clothing. A quick glance told Katerina that she and Katie had little in common.

The bland-looking clothes that hung next to the dark, conservative police uniforms made her want to cry. They were boring as boring could be. What did Katie have against red or orange or bright green?

Katerina yearned to see something vibrant, something that would make her feel connected to this Katie person. She wanted to wear reds, purples, greens and turquoises. She found grays, tans and blues instead.

How could she be so different from the way she was before?

She pulled out a shirt, touched the silky fabric, and raised it against her front. She walked to the floor-length mirror and frowned at her reflection. She looked dull.

A flicker of desperation fueled her sudden anxiety. Fed by a need and fears she couldn't name, she yanked shirts, pants and long dresses from their wire supports.

None of them were familiar. Worst of all, she hated them!

She fought the urge to laugh or howl in frustration.

How could she wear these clothes? They weren't her!

What was she going to do? How could she survive the next few months living in this strange house, married to a man she didn't know and wearing a closet full of clothes that depressed her?

Moisture built at the back of her eyes, but she refused to give in to it. She had to find a way to take control of her life and her future.

She'd ask Mitch if she could buy some new clothes. Clothes that would suit her.

Reaching down to pick-up the pile of clothes she'd rummaged through and discarded, her gaze landed on a long creamy garment tucked in the far end of the closet behind all the other clothes.

A wedding dress.

She stepped over the heap she'd created and reached for the bridal wonder. The gown was carefully cloaked in a clear plastic bag bearing a dry cleaner's name.

Katerina pulled the dress from the back and brought it into the light of the room. She slipped the covering off to see it better. Even to her prejudiced eye, the dress was beautiful. She fingered the satiny, lush cloth.

She recognized the dress as the one Katie had worn in the wedding video. This was the wedding gown.

Katerina didn't give herself time to think. She stripped out of her clothes, unzipped the back of the white garment and stepped into the center.

She didn't look at herself in the mirror until she'd hoisted the sleeves on her arms and fastened the pearl button at the back of the neckline.

Then she slowly walked to the full-length mirror. She

braced herself for what she'd feel and see. The image standing before her didn't look real.

She didn't see Katerina, she saw the ghost of Katie. The sight made her nauseous. With shaking fingers she touched the satiny fabric and tried to remember the other woman.

The dress hugged her perfectly. She recalled the wedding footage and the expression in Mitch's eyes when Katie walked toward him. He'd adored her, making love with his eyes. His emotions hadn't been hidden that day.

He'd loved that woman.

Katerina started to feel closed in. She never felt like such a fraud. Her head swirled with emptiness.

A strangled cough sounded from behind her.

Katerina spun around. Mitch blocked the doorway. In his hand, he clutched a bouquet of white flowers.

Katerina wanted to flee. She'd made a dreadful mistake donning the gown. She wanted to apologize. She wanted to look anywhere except into Mitch's tormented, rigid face. But it was as if her eyes had a will of their own. Her gaze locked on his. His shock pulled at her.

For the life of her she couldn't turn away from his chiseled pain. The raw expression of his face kept her mute and in place. Dark and unsmiling, she saw the feelings he'd kept hidden from her since she'd awaken from the coma. It was all there.

His pain.

His memories.

His unmasked raw desire.

For a woman who no longer existed.

"I'm so sorry," she whispered. "I didn't mean to put it on."

He didn't seem to hear her. "You look beautiful."

It was the last thing she wanted to hear. His hunger

tore at her and mocked her. He was thinking of her. The other her. Katerina felt like the worst type of fraud.

"No. This is a mistake," she pleaded. Couldn't he see? "I'm not her."

Please see me. The real me! The voice inside of her cried. She couldn't release the frozen words from her lips. She could only beg from the depths of her soul that he'd see Katerina, not Katie.

He lifted the bouquet and offered her his gift. "I brought your favorite flowers."

She didn't want to take them. They weren't her favorite flowers.

Then she saw his handle tremble.

Without knowing what to do, she reached out to accept his gift and gathered them close to her. "Thank yo— Achoo!"

Her sudden sneeze startled both of them.

Achoo!

Achoo!

Achoo!

Katerina couldn't catch her breath or stop the itching of her nose. She dropped the flowers. Mitch reached for a tissue on the dresser next to her and thrust it in her hand.

Just as quickly as it started, her nose quit itching.

Katerina wiped the tears from her face. "I don't know what got into me."

Mitch eyed the scattered bouquet at her feet. "You seem to be allergic to the flowers."

She shook her head. "Why would I be?" She started to reach for them, but her nose started to tickle. She sneezed again.

Mitch kicked the offending stems away from her. "Leave them. They're not important."

Katerina managed a tight nod, her heart aching with misery. "I'm sorry. I didn't realize I'd picked up an allergy to boot."

She noticed the remoteness on Mitch's face, all of his emotion wiped clean. "It's not a big deal."

"I'll just change out of this dress," she said.

He didn't seem to hear her. Then he moved. Stooping, Mitch collected the flowers from the floor. "I'll get rid of these and fix something for dinner. Come on, Clancy."

He didn't look back before he closed the door quietly behind him and the dog.

Katerina couldn't escape the confines of the gown fast enough. It was useless to try and dredge up the past through a closet of clothes. The pictures of her past had evaporated as if they never existed. At least for her.

From Mitch's face, she knew they were as real today as they were when they happened.

After she replaced the gown to its corner of the closet, Katerina left the bedroom.

She ventured into the kitchen and found Mitch pulling food from the refrigerator.

"Do you want something to eat?" he asked.

The last thing in the world she wanted was food.

"No, thank you. I'm not very hungry." Her stomach was too full of knots to make room for anything else.

Mitch ignored her response. "You need to eat better." He plied the table with bread, peanut butter, grapes and carrots.

She knew he was hurting. She tried to keep calm. "I'm not hungry."

"Eat something anyway."

She'd endured weeks and weeks of people telling her what to do. She struggled to hold on to her temper.

"Why? Food won't help me remember. That's what you really want, isn't it?"

"Katie…" Then he must have realized how hard and demanding his voice was. He stopped and gave a gusty sigh. "Sorry. I sounded like a nagging parent, didn't I?"

She shook her head. "More like a drill sergeant. I didn't lose my intelligence from the accident. I don't want to be treated like a half-wit."

Her words found their target. Mitch straightened and stood stock-still. She saw his hand curl around the edge of the chair. The only sound came from the kitchen clock ticking by the seconds.

Finally, Mitch unclenched the tight grip he had on the chair. "I'm sorry. That was uncalled for."

She attempted to smile, but her lips were too shaky. "I'm sorry about putting on the wedding dress. I didn't mean to hurt you."

His own attempt at a smile looked just as flat as hers felt.

"It was just a surprise. I'd forgotten the dress was back there."

His face was etched with frustration. He seemed to be at war, but she wasn't sure if it was with her or himself.

He pushed away the food he'd just laid on the counter. "Ever since you woke from the coma, I feel like I'm walking through a minefield," he said. "You've been worried about my expectations of you, but I'm just as confused. I don't know what you expect from me."

His confession startled her and brought her a slight measure of relief. Lines of haggardness made his face look older than it was. Her fingers ached to soothe the weariness. But touching him always distracted her.

She linked her fingers so she wouldn't reach for him. At least Mitch was trying to communicate, even if it wasn't clear what he wanted. "That evens some of the odds," she said quietly. "I don't know what to expect from you, either."

He ran his hand through his thick dark hair, rumpling its usual neatness. He looked more real and approachable to her. "So what do you suggest we do?"

Her fingernails dug into the flesh of her arms. "We just need to learn how to cope with being strangers living in the same house."

"Isn't that what we've been doing?"

"I guess." She looked down at her bloodless fingertips before peering at him through her long eyelashes. "Is it what you want?"

He remained silent for a long moment. "I want both of us to quit being strangers to each other. But I don't know how to do that. I only have the past as a guide. But maybe I didn't know anything then, either."

She sensed his conflicting emotions. The future seemed like an overwhelming long shot for them both. He had the past, but she knew only today. Where was the common ground?

"Perhaps we need to start over and take time to learn about each other," she said slowly, testing the idea in her head at the same time the words exited her mouth. "Like people do when they first meet someone."

"You mean, date each other?" He was facing her fully now and she saw a smidgen of hope flicker in his blue eyes.

She bit her lip. She didn't want to dampen his enthusiasm now that they were broaching an agreement. "I was thinking more in terms of learning to become friends. That's what we're trying to be, isn't it?"

"I don't know if that's possible."

"Weren't we friends before?" she asked.

"Yes—maybe—I don't know. We were married." He sounded irritated.

Katerina nibbled on her lip. He wasn't helping. But she didn't want to give up. "What did you and Katie do? When you were together, I mean."

"We had sex."

His bluntness triggered the blood rushing through her body, making her nipples stand erect. She wished she hadn't started this line of conversation. But now that she had, she couldn't very well stalk from the room. So far every conversation had ended with one of them leaving the room. They had to be able to communicate, no matter what the topic. They needed to be comfortable with each other.

Yet, how comfortable could she be around a man who oozed sensuality from every pore? Even now her pulse was performing a jagged jig. His presence filled the room. The temperature between them was rising.

Out of despair, she made herself pursue the line of questioning. She squared her shoulders and braved his gaze. "What did you and Katie do when you weren't doing that?"

"*We* had more sex."

Images of their naked bodies entwined suddenly rose in her head. Katerina ruthlessly pushed them back and attempted to find a less potent alternative. "Since that activity is not an option now, we'll need to find other ways to start this new friendship. This isn't easy for either of us. But if we can set some guidelines, it'll dispel the awkwardness and tension."

"Are you so unhappy being here?" Mitch asked.

The starkness of his question caused her to react without thinking. "No. I'm not."

She forgot the implicit danger of any rash actions.

Closing the distance between them, she put her hand on his rigid arm muscle. "You have to understand that all this is foreign to me," she said. "I need to be able to find out who I am before I can be someone to anyone else."

"We're married."

"You married another woman." She tried to ignore the heat of his body. "That has no meaning to me. I don't even know you. They're your memories, not mine. What happened before is not a part of who I am now. In my mind, I've never been married. Why can't you see that?"

He sucked in a sharp breath between his teeth. He stared at her hard, as if looking to see a weakness in her stance. She held her head up straight and bore his thorough scrutiny.

"What kind of friendship did you have in mind?" he finally asked.

"I think we need to keep any physical touching at a minimum."

When his gaze dropped to her arm, she guiltily raised her hand from his arm and stepped back. She didn't buckle under his darkening expression, but plunged ahead. "No kissing. No touching. No sexual expectations."

"What can we do?"

She offered him a smile. "We might plan some activities."

"Like what?"

She had to think fast. "Bike riding. I'd like to see if I could ride a bike."

"Bike riding?" He choked on the word. "I haven't ridden a bike in years. I doubt if I even remember how."

His incredulous response made her grin and feel

bolder. "Then we can learn together, and I won't feel like I'm such an oddball."

His gaze glinted. The light caught the glittery grays feathered throughout his dark head of hair. "Who says you're an oddball?"

She nodded toward Dog. "Have you any idea what it's like to have a dog look at you with misery in his eyes because you can't throw him a football?"

Mitch started to chuckle. The sound started out softly and then filled the room.

The freedom of his laughter made Katerina's heart pick up a beat.

Mitch pulled her hand that had been resting on his forearm to his chest, where she could feel the rumbling of his heartbeat. The warmth of his skin through his shirt tugged at her and made her feel all tingly inside.

"I can't smell, I can't taste. I can't even remember half of what I did a few minutes ago."

"You're not an oddball, Katie. You just put a different spin on what the rest of us take for granted. It makes you special," he said after his laughter died away.

"Does it? Am I special?" She couldn't stop the bud of hope rising inside her.

He held her gaze. "You don't have to be like everyone else. Why not just enjoy being yourself?"

Did he really care for her as she was? She searched his face for the answer.

"We'll take it a day at a time." He tugged her arm closer to his heart. She could feel his pounding heartbeat through the thickness of his clothing. "I can't say I won't touch you. Even friends touch each other. Besides, I look forward to those spontaneous caresses of yours. They give me hope." He stroked his thumb over the sensitive skin of her wrist, playing havoc with her pulse. "But I will promise that I won't do anything you don't want me to.''

The intensity of his gaze on hers made her throat constrict. She saw the sincerity and the desire within his dark pupils. Suddenly she felt a strange sensation in her midsection. To cover her confusion, she looked down at the hand that covered hers. His skin was tanned and warm. Hers appeared white and cool. They were so different. Yet, it did feel good and right to be close to him this way.

She nibbled on the inside of her cheek.

He placed his hand under her chin and lifted it so she met his eyes. ''We can work this out.''

When she was this close to him she had trouble thinking. She had a crazy desire to break her new rules and slip into his arms. It took all of her willpower to stay where she was. ''How can you be so sure?'' she asked.

''You're still Katie. A head injury can't change that.''

''I don't even know what you and I did when we were in this room the last time together.''

''Do you want me to tell you?''

The swirling depths of his seductive gaze warned her. She wanted to shout yes. She wanted to know everything he could teach her and then some. But what would happen then? Would he regret having made love to a woman with Katie's face, but who was no longer his beloved wife?

Katerina licked her lips. ''Maybe it would be best if you told me about my hobbies instead.''

''Yeah, that would be best,'' he said, but he didn't look convinced. He seemed to be weighing something heavy in his mind.

''Is there something wrong?''

He tried to smooth down his hair. ''I was wondering

if you'd given any more thought to giving this marriage a go?''

His question pricked her heart. She couldn't find her breath, let alone her voice. She didn't know how to answer him.

Was he asking her to love him?

No, he hadn't mentioned anything about love. Neither had he confessed to loving her. This was strictly about marriage. A part of her badly wanted to say yes. It would be so easy to step into another woman's shoes and take over her life. Where else could she find such a strong, dependable, good-looking man?

But the practical side of her knew that she'd be living a lie. What looked easy and seductive could lead to heartache.

''Do you think you could look at me and not see Katie?'' she asked.

She saw his eyes sweep her from head to toe. The light of expectation dimmed from his face. ''I don't know.'' His hoarse reply couldn't mask the bleakness in his gaze.

She had her answer. And he had his.

''I think we'll have to settle for friendship.''

His jaw squared. ''At least for now.''

# Chapter 6

Mitch didn't sleep well that night, which didn't surprise him in the least. He was too damn conscious of the fact that Katie was just down the hall. He missed having her body curled up next to his. They'd fit together perfectly.

The memories she'd lost tormented him.

Before he was married, he'd been an early-morning riser. But that had changed as soon as they married. He found it harder and harder to pull away from his wife's arms in the morning. When they were in bed together, the rest of the world couldn't come between them. They were cocooned in their own nest, untouched by the realities of jobs, schedules and other people.

Everything in this room reminded him of his wife and the dreams he'd woven from the moment they'd first met. Her unique scent clung to her pillow, and he hated the chilly emptiness of the sheets on her side of the bed. He'd thought nothing could be worse than life without her.

He'd been wrong. Having Katie here in the house and not being able to touch her was a hell of a lot worse.

He managed to get through his early morning chores without falling asleep behind the wheel of his tractor. He figured God was watching over him for a change. After he met with Toby, one of the farm hands, and gave him instructions for the day, Mitch went into the house for breakfast.

He found Katie rummaging through a trunk of old clothes in the guest room.

"What are you looking for?"

Katie glared at him from over her shoulder. "Didn't she wear anything besides drab tans and brown?"

He frowned. "You don't like the colors of the clothes?"

"I look like a corpse."

She pulled out a pair of iridescent green pants and frowned at them critically. "These have possibilities."

Mitch cocked his eyebrow. When had he seen those pants before? "Aren't those part of a Halloween costume?"

She sighed. "Too bad they aren't bright orange. Orange is a good color for me."

Mitch wasn't sure if she was joking or not, but the deep pucker between her eyebrows told him she was dead serious. She wanted colorful clothes and wasn't going to be happy with anything less. Eyeing the ridiculous costume she was considering, he made a decision. "Why don't we go shopping for some new clothes?"

She lowered the clownish pants, her expression beamed with hope. "Really? When?"

He shrugged. "We're going to town for your doctor's appointment. If we leave in a half hour, we can check out the stores before I drop you at the clinic."

A smile transformed her face. She looked the happiest he'd seen her since she'd been home. As quickly as she could, she stuffed the costume back into the trunk. Then she sprang to her feet and reached up to give him a kiss on the cheek.

Before he could react, she had slipped out of his range and was heading down the hall. "I'll wait in the car until you're ready."

He gulped a sigh. Damn! If he'd known he was going to get that kind of response for offering a shopping trip, he'd have taken her to town directly from the hospital.

He couldn't stop the surge of optimism. Yesterday he'd been sure his marriage was lost for good. She hadn't even been willing to consider making the union work after the fiasco with the wedding dress.

He thought he'd blown his chances for sure. When he'd seen her standing there, every inch the bride he remembered marrying, he hadn't been able to think of anything else but making their vows real again. It had taken all of his willpower to resist the urge to throw her down on the bed and make her his again. He didn't know what had restrained him.

He ached in every way possible for a man to ache for a woman.

Perhaps it had been the wariness in her eyes.

Or perhaps his own dreaded fear that if they did make love, he could scare her away for good. Lord knew he wanted her so much that he wouldn't be able to take it slow. He'd probably terrorize her.

He wondered if there would ever be a time he could? Would they ever again fall naturally into each other's arms? His only chance to make that happen was to discover who his wife really was.

Somehow he was going to have to find a way to court

Katie into being his wife again. He had trouble recognizing her since her head injury, but she was still the woman for him. He knew that on the deepest gut level.

If he could just find out a way to make her fall in love with him again.

Buying a new wardrobe of clothes could be the start. It was an unusual way to start a courtship, but then, most dating didn't start after the rings had been exchanged and the vows were three years old.

He had no rules to guide him. He'd just have to follow his instincts and hope he got a bit of luck along the way.

Mitch walked to the open trunk and stared down at the Halloween costume that had captured Katie's attention and enthusiasm. Remembering her rapt expression, he shook his head.

If nothing else, taking his wife shopping should prove to be very enlightening.

He glanced down at the blinding garment one more time. Mitch hoped he had the stomach for this adventure. He had a feeling he was going to need a strong constitution to see this day through.

Going through the racks and racks of clothes, Katerina refused to consider anything pastel or the color of dirt. The salesclerk was quickly able to discern that "dirt" colors meant anything that wasn't piping pink, flaming red or neon blue. Katie turned her back on the hangers of khaki pants and casual denims. She equally dismissed a black knit top and forest-green blouse as being too dull.

She plucked an orange wraparound skirt and crimson-rose top from the clearance rack. A sassy short yellow dress and blinding blue top earned a squeal and a dimple. Mitch might have been horrified at her choice, but he couldn't say no to that smile. Katie had become Katie again. And if she wanted to wear a bold red T-shirt, a flashy purple pair of socks and glittery striped scarf, he was all for it.

"Your wife has very strong tastes," the salesclerk said to him when Katie trotted into the dressing room.

"She seems to," Mitch replied.

"Most women around aren't brave enough to go against the arch conservatism. Their menfolk are too picky. But your wife is a woman who knows what she likes no matter what anyone else thinks. She knows you'll love anything she likes. I wish more men were like you." There was a note of envy in the young clerk's voice.

Mitch didn't want to burst her bubble and tell her he always favored conservative styles.

But he couldn't help wondering if Katie had dressed to please him or herself?

If there had always been this side of Katie, why hadn't he seen it before? He didn't like the idea that he'd in some way been responsible for Katie's choosing clothes she didn't care for.

"What do you think?" Katie came out of the dressing room and twirled in front of him. Her green eyes positively danced as she pivoted.

Mitch swallowed hard as he looked at the sexy image in front of him. Thinking wasn't an option at the moment. Katie wore that sassy yellow dress. It came a good six inches above her knees and showed off her legs beautifully. Mitch's body reacted instantaneously. He didn't dare move for fear he'd draw attention to his arousal.

He reached for the newspaper on the table next to him and casually draped it across his lap.

When he realized Katie was looking at him with expectation, he said, "It looks nice."

"It does, doesn't it?" Katie didn't seem to notice his discomfort.

"It looks better than fine," the young clerk chimed in. "That outfit is divine on you."

Her enthusiasm earned her the full beam of Katie's smile. "Do you think so?"

"I only wish I could wear that color," the young girl said wistfully.

Katie stopped her twirling. "Why can't you?"

"My boyfriend hates anything bright. He says I look like a hooker. You're so lucky to have a man who isn't worried about you attracting other men."

Katie's questioning gaze sought Mitch's. "Do you think this is too bright?"

Mitch would have cut out his tongue rather than dash her enthusiasm. "No, I agree with our young friend here. The dress is divine."

Katie tilted her head and stared into his face, as if she wasn't sure she could believe him. Was she questioning his truthfulness or was she seeing something in him she hadn't seen before?

Mitch returned her gaze. What he saw deflated the air from his lungs. He'd wanted to seduce and court his wife. But he was the one being seduced. Awareness throbbed between them. He saw it in the way her lips parted and her eyes widened. He'd bet money on the fact that even though she couldn't see below the newspaper, she knew he was aroused.

Finally her face underwent another transformation, softening. The corners of her mouth quivered. "I'm glad you like it."

"I do." His words were so low that only Katie heard them. Did she understand he approved of more than just the garment she wore?

"Are you going to try on the other outfits, miss?" the girl asked.

Katie didn't meet Mitch's gaze, but a shade of pink seeped across her face. "Yes. I believe I will."

Forty-five minutes later Mitch handed over his charge card to pay for Katie's purchases, even though he wasn't sure Bakerstown was ready for the new Katie and her exuberant wardrobe.

The clothes were neatly packaged in large department store bags, except for the yellow dress, which Katie had decided to wear. They'd also bought her a new red coat to wear over the dress. The March air contained a nippy chill, and Mitch didn't want her dying of exposure—at least that was his excuse for insisting she cover her leggy limbs. She wore nude panty hose that made her legs looked naked. Mitch wondered if he dared leave her alone.

After they loaded up the car, he turned down Main Street toward the clinic.

"Do you want me to come in with you?" he asked, parking in front of the doctor's office.

Katerina shook her head. She was feeling decidedly vulnerable since she'd left the store. She had the strong urge to put some distance between her and her husband. Thinking was hard for her to do under the best of circumstances. Right now, all she could do was react to the overwhelming feeling of having Mitch so close. Something seemed to be changing between them.

She wanted time to regroup and gather her thoughts.

However, when she walked into the office a few minutes later, the receptionist at the desk gave her an apologetic smile. "I'm sorry, Mrs. Reeves, I've been trying to call you. Dr. Norton had an emergency and won't be in for several hours. We had to cancel your appointment.''

Katerina frowned. "We came to town early and did some shopping."

The woman behind the desk eyed her colorful outfit. "That must be new. It's sensational."

Katerina recognized the same note of wistfulness in her voice as that of the young store clerk's. "Thank you," Katerina said. She turned and looked at the empty chairs behind her.

"Do you need to call your husband to come and get you?"

Katerina had no idea where Mitch had gone. She'd been in such a hurry to escape his presence, she hadn't asked. He had promised to be back in an hour. "No, that's not necessary," she said. Then a thought occurred to her. "Could you tell me how far the police department is from here?"

"It's just down the street." The receptionist pointed over Katerina's shoulder. "Go out the door and take a right. You'll see the department's sign."

"Will you tell my husband where I went if he returns before I do?" Katerina asked.

"Sure I will," the older woman replied.

The phone started to ring, and the receptionist was talking into the mouthpiece as Katie left the building.

Katerina kept repeating the directions so she wouldn't get confused or lost. Fortunately, the department's sign was easy to spot.

She pulled open the big glass doors and walked through two metal detectors.

"Good afternoon, Katie." A uniformed security guard smiled at her as she walked up the stairs.

"Hi." She didn't recognize him, but that didn't surprise her any longer. "I'm sorry, but I don't remember…"

"I'm Hank."

She nodded. "Hank. It's nice to meet you."

"You're a sight for sore eyes. The place hasn't been the same since you—" He stopped, his eyes widening with consternation as he suddenly realized his gaffe.

She reached over and patted his sleeve. "It's nice to be missed, even if I don't remember."

He blinked rapidly as if he had something in his eye. "Don't pay attention to me," he said gruffly. "You just gave us such a terrific scare. I'm relieved to see you walking and talking."

"I'm glad to be walking and talking, too."

He gestured up the stairs. "They'll all be glad you're here. Rafe has been real cranky since you left."

"Could you show me the way?"

Before he could answer, a voice boomed down the stairwell. "Well, as I live and breathe, if it isn't our missing detective." Rafe Henderson came down two steps at a time. His wide shoulders and boisterous voice took over the entire stairwell.

Katerina didn't have time to answer as several other officers came up behind them.

One of them cuffed her shoulder affectionately. "Hey, it's about time you quit taking vacation, Reeves."

Another threw an arm over her shoulder. "Have you gotten tired of the easy life and decided to come back to work?"

Their faces were familiar, even though she couldn't recall any of their names. They must have visited her in the hospital.

"Get away, you dogs," Rafe snarled. "She came to see me, not you."

"Says who?" the guy with his arm around her shoulder countered.

"Says me. I'm her partner."

"No wonder she lost her memory," the other man muttered loud enough for everyone to hear.

Everyone around them started to laugh.

"Hey, Katie, want to help me with a ten-thirty?"

"Ten-thirty?" she asked, wondering if she'd heard him right.

"Yep, we've got a robbery in progress at the—"

"Hey, who made you captain?" someone else protested. "She can assist with the ten-thirty-four. A woman is always an asset with assault cases, and Katie is the best."

Katerina's head whirled with confusion from the strange faces to the foreign-sounding lingo. Yet, she felt surprisingly comfortable. They could have made her feel awkward and out of place, but there was a genuine warmth and caring from the people crowding close to her.

"My gosh, you toads. Let the woman breathe, for heaven's sake." Mandy Vincent shooed them back. Katerina was relieved to recognize the female detective who had visited the farm with Rafe. The detective pushed her way toward Katerina's side. "Give her a chance to breathe."

"That's right. You guys back off. Katie's my partner," Rafe added.

Mandy ignored him and gave Katerina's arm a friendly squeeze. "I'm really glad you stopped by."

Katerina went with the flow of bodies. "The doctor had an emergency, so I didn't have my appointment."

"Would you like the grand tour or just to see your desk?"

Katie was beginning to feel overloaded. "I'd like to

see my desk. Perhaps you can show me the rest of the building later.''

''No problem.''

They walked into a room littered with desks, computer terminals and files of every shape and size. There were phones ringing and people talking. A few people raised hands of greeting as she walked by their desks. She answered with a smile and nodded as Mandy filled in names that Katerina knew she'd forget by the time she got to her desk.

''Here it is. Home sweet home.'' Rafe pulled out a chair for her.

Katerina sat in the tweed covered chair and eyed the wide empty desk. The computer screen was turned off. A picture of Mitch sat in the corner next to a pencil holder. Other than that, the desk was bare.

''Well, look who's here,'' a man said from behind her.

She swiveled the chair and saw a wavy gray-haired man bearing down on her.

''It's Captain Loomis,'' Mandy murmured for Katerina's ears.

The older man looked fit and trim. He wore a stern expression that was lightened by teasing eyes. ''Does this mean you're ready to start punching the clock again?'' he asked.

''Just as soon as the doctor says the word,'' she replied gamely.

He nodded. ''Good. We can use you around here. These slackers don't seem to be able to get anything done since you've been out.''

Rafe folded his arms. ''We've gotten plenty of things done. You just haven't been reading our reports.''

The captain frowned. ''I can't read your spelling, Henderson. Since Reeves has been gone, I've been able to read my grandson's first-grade penmanship easier than your scratchings.''

"Hey, it isn't that bad.''

"Yes, it is,'' Mandy interjected.

The playful poking and teasing around Katerina made her feel as though she was one of them. Yet underneath she sensed their professionalism. She noticed that each time a phone rang, a subtle signal of alert went through the room. Each officer kept an eye on the door and kept track of the comings and goings.

As easy as they made it for her to slip into her desk, she didn't have a clue as to what was going on, or who did what.

"Hey, Captain, phone call from the mayor,'' someone called across the room.

"I'll take it in my office,'' the captain said. He pressed Katerina's shoulder comfortingly. "When you feel you're ready, give me a call and we'll talk.''

Although she nodded and gave him a smile, inside she knew that they'd have little to talk about because she didn't even understand their language. As welcoming as the police officers were, she no longer had the skills the job demanded. The lingo between officers was as foreign to her as if they'd been speaking Russian.

Katerina started to turn the seat of her chair back to the desk, when her leg nudged against something decidedly human.

She pulled back.

Inside the alcove where her legs should be, a little boy crouched with his legs drawn up to his chin.

Rafe sauntered around the corner with Mandy.

"Hi, there, Jacob.'' The big man's voice had lost its booming edge. He didn't try to touch the child as the boy drew himself deeper into the corner. "Does your grandma know you're here?"

"She'll be here soon," Mandy murmured.

Katerina could see the stark fear peeking from beneath the small boy's dark brown bangs. He had a slight build and seemed to be small for his age. His ancient eyes were an oddity on his young face. They were as old as old can be.

She got lost in the swell of need and desperation in his wide, expressive gaze. She hunkered to his level and slid in close to him, without touching him. "This is a rather cozy spot, isn't it?" she asked.

The boy didn't speak, but she thought she saw a glimmer of interest in the depths of his brown eyes.

She continued as if they were carrying on a conversation. "The world looks more manageable from here. No one can catch you blindsided."

The boy stared hard at her. She wished she knew what he was thinking.

When her legs started to cramp, she asked him, "Don't you want to come out?"

The boy still didn't respond. If anything, he scooted tighter into his corner.

"Has anyone called his grandmother?" said one of the other officers.

"How does he get in here? Where's our security?"

"The captain figures Hank is looking the other way when the kid comes through the door. Hank has a soft spot for little kids. He's a grandfather three times over."

"That kid has a load on his mind."

Katie heard the conversation, but she didn't lift her head or break her eye contact with the boy. He wanted something from her. She could feel the silent messages he was sending her. What did they mean? What had he seen?

She searched for something to say. To break through the wall he'd built around himself. Her gaze flickered over his neat attire. He wore a green Packers jacket with blue jeans.

"I like your jacket. Did your grandma buy you that?" she asked.

He lifted his head a bit, looking wary. Then he slowly nodded his head.

"Hallelujah. Would you look at that?" Rafe said. "The kid is responding."

Katerina never lost her concentration. She pointed to the high-top tennis shoes. "I'll bet those are new sneakers, aren't they?"

Again the child in the cubbyhole nodded. But he didn't move from his cramped quarters. She reached a hand toward him. "Would you like to come out so we could talk and get to know each other?"

He seemed unsure. His eyes flickered to the people standing behind her.

"They won't hurt you," she said softly. She wished she could remember his name, but as usual her memory hadn't held on to that little fact. "They just want to make sure you're okay. Come out, honey. I won't let anyone hurt you."

His eyes contained a curious light as she talked to him. He carefully unlocked his hands from around his knees and placed his small fingers in her hand. She tugged him gently forward, and he crept out of his hiding place. Almost eagerly.

The officers stepped back giving them some room as Katerina stayed at his level. The boy stared at her, a trace of hope in his expression.

She smiled encouragingly.

Then he reached up and touched her head. He unerringly found the very spot where she'd hit her head. She saw the question in his face. "Did you hear about my accident?"

He stroked her face but didn't respond.

"It's almost healed," she told him. "I have a hard head. I'm surprised there isn't a big hole where my head hit."

He pulled his hand back, not looking convinced.

"Maybe Jacob would like a can of soda," Mandy whispered to her.

"Would you like a can of soda?" Katerina asked.

The boy's mouth crept slowly into a smile.

"I guess that means yes," Katerina said.

"What kind would you like, boy? I'll get it," Rafe offered.

The boy's gaze went from longing to despair.

Katerina saw his frustration and gazed up at Rafe. "What kind do you have?"

"Root beer, orange, grape, cola."

Katerina lifted Jacob's hand. "Squeeze my hand when I say the kind you'd prefer. Root beer, orange, grape or cola."

He squeezed her fingers for grape.

After Rafe left to get the soda, the other officers dispersed to their desks. Only Mandy hovered in the background.

Katerina wasn't sure what to do. She finally went with her instincts and did what felt natural. She sat at her desk, which put her at eye level with the boy. "Would you like to help me look through my desk, honey?"

He nodded. She slid over to make room for the child to sit next to her. She wished she knew what she could do to help the little boy. Unfortunately she didn't have a single recollection of either him or the accident that had claimed his mother's life.

She pulled open the desk drawer to reveal several sharpened pencils lined up in the front. Behind the pencil tray were two file folders and a small stack of plain paper.

"Would you like to draw something?" she asked.

Before he could answer, the door opened and a harried, short woman in her fifties rushed in. As soon as she spotted the boy, she placed her hand across her chest in relief. "Oh, thank God. Jacob, there you are."

Worry mingled with the frustration in the older woman's face. Katerina noticed she seemed genuinely distraught and relieved at the same time.

The door she had come through swung open again. This time Katerina saw Mitch's large frame step into the room. His arrival was greeted with nods from several occupants. Katerina felt the atmosphere become closer. It was amazing no one else noticed the barometric changes.

From across the room, Mitch's gaze found hers. Was he unhappy she'd come here? She couldn't decipher his thoughts any more than she could the little boy's.

Mitch seemed to instantly understand the drama taking place before him. He stayed back as the child, oblivious to his arrival and anyone else's presence, ran into his grandmother's arms, allowing her to hug him tight.

"You had me so worried." Her scold was softened by her fevered kisses against his hair. "Why did you slip out of the yard, Jacob?"

Jacob buried his face into her skirt, hiding his thoughts and secrets.

Rafe slipped into their tight circle. "Here's your soda, son."

The boy looked at his grandmother for permission. She

hesitated only briefly. "Okay, you can have it. But I expect you to eat all of your supper when we get home."

Katerina made room on her chair for Jacob to sit again. While he drank his soda, the grandmother gestured to Rafe and Mandy. They moved into another cubicle. Even though they lowered their voices, Katerina could hear the grandmother's agitation. "I think there's someone calling our house."

"What make's you think that?" Mandy asked.

"I've been getting phone calls, and no one is there. I can hear someone breathing on the other end. I know this has something to do with the accident. Jacob runs into his room and hides under the bed when the phone rings. I was hanging the clothes on the line today. When I came in, he was gone."

"Do you think he answered the phone while you were out?"

"I don't know."

The despair in the grandmother's voice tugged at Katerina. The woman's voice dipped, and Katerina could no longer discern the details of their conversation.

She felt Jacob's stillness at her side. "Would you like to draw a picture?" she asked him.

He shook his head. She noticed that he sat sideways and kept a close eye on the door. Whenever anyone came into the room, he shrank against her until the person moved out of range.

Looking across the room, she saw Mitch watching them. He seemed puzzled by the boy's attachment to her, but he didn't try to interfere.

"Jacob, we need to go home. Our dinner is baking in the oven," his grandmother said as she came around the cubicle.

The boy didn't argue. He slipped his hand in the older

woman's grasp. With the other, he clutched his soda can. He turned to look at Katerina one more time.

"It's nice meeting you, honey," she said. His name slipped her mind as quickly as it had appeared.

He gave her a wide smile before leaving the room.

Rafe leaned against her desk. "What did you think of him?"

Katerina lifted her shoulders helplessly. "He seems lonely and afraid."

Rafe sighed. "Yeah, but what's he afraid of? That's the million-dollar question."

"Why does he come here?" Mandy added. "He always watches the door, as if he's looking for someone."

"His grandmother seems worried," Katerina said.

"Yeah. We'll send a car over to keep a close watch on the neighborhood. But for all we know, it could be someone who wants to buy property."

At Rafe's comment, Mitch moved forward. "Katie and I will leave you to figure it out. We need to get home so I can start chores."

Katerina stood. She gave the detectives a warm smile. "Thank you for allowing me to visit. I'm sorry I wasn't able to help."

Rafe shook his head. "I wouldn't be too sure of that. We've never been able to coax that kid out from under your desk before. He stays there until his grandmother tracks him down. Whatever the reason, he trusts you. That's a start."

Mandy echoed her partner's sentiments. "Rafe is right. You helped. Communicating with him was a major breakthrough."

"Now we need to get him to communicate with us. We're just not sure how we can do that."

Mitch nudged Katerina gently toward the door. But she

stopped beside Mandy. "Will you keep me posted about the boy?" she asked.

"Count on it."

Mitch pulled open the door and Katerina found herself outside the building.

The sun seemed warm, but she couldn't still the chill from her bones.

Katerina wasn't sure if it was Mitch's tight expression or the worry she had for the little boy. But even her new dress didn't lift her spirits.

## Chapter 7

Mitch didn't give Katie time for a long goodbye. He purposefully steered her toward the door and out of the building before the detectives could drag her into the investigation they were working on. For once, Katie didn't question him.

She was curiously quiet until they reached the car. That bothered him more than he liked to admit. He'd gotten used to being the recipient of her flow of consciousness. Her silence made him uneasy.

He started to turn the key in the ignition when she reached over and touched his arm. Mitch went still at the feel of her cool fingers against his flesh, bringing an instant response from other parts of his body. There had been too many long days and endless nights without her.

"I'm sorry I didn't wait for you at the doctor's office," she said. "But I was curious about the police department and what my old job was like."

Mitch shrugged. "The receptionist told me about the hospital emergency and where you were."

She lifted her fingers from his arm and he was able to breathe again. Backing the car away from the building, he headed toward home.

Katie absently rubbed her scar. "He's such a cute little boy, isn't he?"

"Yeah." Mitch didn't want to think about the little boy and his needs. But the kid's face lingered clearly in his mind's eye.

"What is his name?" she asked.

"Jacob."

"Jacob. Jacob. Jacob," she repeated with a determined note to her tone. "I need to remember his name. He's already lost so much."

Mitch remembered the longing he saw on the little guy's face. He could relate too easily to the intense adoration the kid bestowed on Katie. "I don't think he'll hold it against you if you don't recall his name."

"No, but his name is all he has left, isn't it?"

"He has his grandmother. He has a home."

Mitch took his eyes off the road briefly and saw the sadness flicker across Katie's expression. She had absorbed the boy's loss and made it her own.

"It's not the same as having a mother. I don't know what I would have done if I'd lost mine. Mothers should be for always."

"That depends on the mother." The words came out of his mouth before he could stop them.

"What happened to your mother?" Katie asked, as he knew she would.

Discussing his mother and his childhood wasn't a topic of conversation he ever introduced, much less enjoyed.

His past was a part of him, a part he preferred to keep buried. Yet Katie's interest was a good sign.

"My mother worked herself to death," he said, hoping his judgment didn't show.

"How did she do that?"

"She just kept working, ignoring the signs that she needed to take care of other parts of her life. Eventually her heart gave out."

"She put herself ahead of you?"

He shrugged. "Usually."

"How old were you?"

His answers didn't abbreviate her curiosity.

"Sixteen."

He heard her sharp intake of breath. "That's so young. You were just a little boy. Almost like…like Jacob."

"Not exactly. Jacob had a mother. My mother was never there. It's different when someone chooses to not be with you. I've been on my own for years. The only thing that changed when my mother died was that I didn't have to leave a light on for her when I went to bed."

Mitch found it easier to pretend it happened to someone else. That had been the key. In his case, he pretended he never had a mother even when she was alive. What you never had, you never missed.

"I'm sorry," she said.

He swallowed. "Don't be. You can't miss what you never have."

She was silent for a few miles, an unusual allotment of time for her. "I'm never going to let that happen."

He glanced at her. "What happen?"

"I'm never going to put a job ahead of my child."

She said it so ferociously he couldn't help but want to believe her.

Mitch felt the tension building inside him. How he

would like to believe that. "Sometimes people do it despite their best intentions."

"Maybe that's what happened with your mother. She didn't realize how much you needed her."

He hadn't thought about his mother in years. When he did, he never considered his home life from his mother's point of view. "The only person who can answer that is dead."

Above the sound of the tires humming along the pavement, Katerina heard his deep pain tangled with doubt. How could a mother not love a child? Especially someone as steady and caring as Mitch. Every child needed to know he was loved and cherished. Katerina had an urgent need to mend his heart even if she didn't completely understand his hurt.

"I'm sure she loved you very much," she said with conviction.

Mitch didn't want to discuss his mother any longer. He knew that nothing could change his childhood, or his mother's actions. He chose to divert Katie's attention. "You had a good mother. She didn't leave you home to fend for yourself."

Katerina shook her head. "No, she didn't. My father was gone so much she didn't feel she could have a career." Some of her childhood was clear in her head. Other pictures were hazy and vague. She had trouble recalling her father's face. It was as if time and distance had made those images blurry. She loved her father, but she couldn't remember doing a lot with him. "My mother always said that Dad showed his love by his commitment to his job."

Mitch took his eyes off the road briefly. "As a kid, you probably didn't understand his absence any more than I understood my mother's."

"That's probably why I wanted to be a detective. To feel closer to my father," she mused. She saw the trees go by on the side of the road. But the size and shape were mere impressions. They passed by in a whirl.

"What about now?" he asked.

"Now?"

"How do you feel about being a detective?"

She thought his voice sounded tight and strained. Given his distant relationship with his mother, she could understand his trepidation.

"I don't know," she answered as honestly as she could.

She recognized the tall silos in the distance. They were approaching the boundary of Mitch's land. "If I worked, I'd want to do something that was right for me, not because of my parents. The nurse at the hospital told me nothing could be more rewarding than to help another human being. I'd like to help that little boy." She turned to him. "Wouldn't you help him if you could?"

Mitch didn't respond. She noticed his brow furrow into deep thought, as if he were holding his thoughts tightly inside.

Katerina ran her hands along the leathered armrest and thought about Jacob. But then her mind shifted. Jacob's boyish countenance changed into Mitch's. She could almost picture his beautiful blue eyes on a small, solemn face. A son of Mitch's would be intense. How she'd love to see that face alight with mischief and laughter. Not sober and scared like Jacob's. Not adult-like, with too much responsibility and burden for his years.

"I need to learn how to throw a ball," she announced out of the blue.

The furrows left Mitch's face as his mouth curved upward. "You're still bothered by Clancy's reaction, aren't you?"

Katerina heard humor in his voice. She turned her head and eyed him suspiciously. "You're laughing at my ball-throwing skills."

He pulled the car up in front of the house and parked it. As soon as he cut the engine, he turned. The sizzling blue of his gaze found her. "No, I'm sharing a special moment with you."

When he looked at her that way, her screwy brain went even screwier. She felt suddenly light-headed and happy.

"I wish—" she stopped, fearing if she said what she desired, she'd ruin the moment.

Mitch touched one of the freckles on her nose. "What do you wish?"

"I don't know," she said helplessly.

His gaze mesmerized hers, going from stormy blue to the color of the sky. "Do you know what I wish?"

She shook her head.

"I wish I could be in Jacob's shoes," he said simply.

Her mouth dropped open. "Why?"

"Because even though he lost his mother, he's already got you for a champion."

Her eyes widened with distress. "How is that a benefit? I don't even know if I can help him."

"Yes, you can. You've already proved it."

"How?"

"You remembered his name."

"Jacob. His name is Jacob."

"See what I mean? Once you put your mind to something, you're a force to be reckoned with. What more could he ask for?"

Mitch's voice thickened with emotion. Katerina couldn't control the shiver that swept through her body.

She wasn't sure if it was because of the heat she saw in his eyes, or the chill brought on by the setting sun. She only knew that she craved a warmth that was eluding her.

"We'd better get you inside."

Before she could respond, Mitch opened the car door. The blast of early evening air made her shiver again.

Her mind whirled with muddled impressions as he came around to her side of the vehicle. She couldn't begin to decipher the meaning of their conversation. But one thing she knew, she'd glimpsed Mitch's softer side. What she hadn't suspected was how much more seductive that side was to her sanity.

She not only suspected he'd be a terrific father; he'd also be a terrific husband and lover.

How had Katie ever left his bed? The woman had to have been plumb out of her mind.

Katerina chalked up one more difference between her and the other woman.

She'd never leave Mitch for a job, or anything else. If he loved her and she loved him, she'd fight everyone and everything to keep them together.

And she'd do everything to make Mitch's life whole again.

Katerina's fierce reaction to his desolate childhood and his loneliness made her recognize a commonality between them. Mitch knew what it was to be different from everyone else. She'd seen the expression in his face when he'd looked at Jacob. There was an understanding there.

Katerina's fingers curled, her fingernails digging into her tender palms. She wanted to comfort him. She wanted to give him what had been taken away.

But would he want it?

She wasn't the woman he wanted, or needed—even though he kept saying they were the same.

She had no way of changing who she was or who he was.

Still, she wanted to give him something. He'd done a lot for her.

She owed him.

"Do you like chili?" she asked as soon as they stepped into the house.

Mitch frowned. "You want me to fix chili for dinner?"

"No, I'm going to fix it for you."

He'd seemed distracted. Now, she'd caught his full attention. His expression bore a distinct uneasiness. "I don't think—"

She waved her hand. "Go do your chores, and I'll have it ready when you get in. I have a marvelous recipe from my cooking class. Everyone raved about it."

She reached for the timer above the stove. Part of her rehabilitation had been learning how to cook and work with a timer. Her short-term memory lapses were a challenge in the kitchen, but she had been determined to master those skills she'd lost. Now would be a good time to demonstrate her abilities.

"Are you sure you don't need some help?" Mitch asked.

"No." She was already trying to commit to memory all the ingredients for the recipe. "Just give me a time when I should have it ready."

"I'll try to be in by eight o'clock."

She set her timer. "Eight o'clock it is."

Dog kept close to Katerina's side after Mitch left. She compiled the ingredients, keeping close track of each item so as not to forget where she was.

She was getting ready to add a tablespoon of chili powder when the phone interrupted her.

"Katerina, it's Mother."

Katerina juggled the receiver to her ear, while stirring the soup. "Hi, Mother. How are you doing?"

"Better. The doctor thinks I'll be able to travel in a couple of months. Duane and I are planning to drive up for the Fourth of July."

"That's great."

"You sound distracted."

Katerina stared at the measuring spoon in her hand. Had she added the chili powder or not? She couldn't recall; she'd added several seasonings. Were the speckles in the measuring spoon from the seasoning or the chili powder? "I'm just cooking Mitch dinner."

"What are you preparing?"

"Chili."

"Are you using my recipe?" her mother asked.

"No, it's one I got from the class."

"Oh. Well, don't forget to add enough seasoning and spice. That's the secret to good chili."

Katerina frowned. "All right." Had she added the chili powder or not?

"I won't keep you," her mother said. "Why don't you call me tomorrow?"

Katerina's goodbye was distracted as she cradled the receiver.

"Did I add the chili powder or not, Dog?" she asked the companion at her side.

The canine wagged his tail and nuzzled close. He, no doubt, was begging for a handout.

Katerina sighed. "You're not much help."

She stared at the mixture. Everything looked fine. The color appeared a little pale, however. Obviously she hadn't added the chili. She carefully measured a full tablespoon.

The dratted phone interrupted her.

Should she answer it or not? She didn't want to lose her place in the recipe again.

The noisy instrument shrilled again. Dog whined.

Katerina grabbed the offensive machine.

"Katerina?"

"Yes?"

"This is Dr. Norton's office. We wanted to reschedule your appointment. Do you think you could come in on Friday?"

"Friday?" Katerina pushed the recipe book aside, accidentally knocking the measuring spoon into the sink.

As the spoon sank into the dish water, Katerina grappled to hang on to the receiver and keep calm.

She found the calendar tucked under her recipe book and perused the dates. "Friday should be fine," she told the woman on the other end.

"I'll write you down. If there's a problem, just give us a call."

The interruption ended as abruptly as it started. Katerina made a note on the calendar.

Dog nudged her leg. Katerina looked down at him and saw his nose quiver toward the stove.

"Oh, the chili." She reached over and grabbed her spoon to stir the sizzling mixture.

Her heart raced as she spotted the container of chili powder perched next to the stove. She'd been adding ingredients to the meat, but where had she left off? Had she added the chili powder or not?

She sniffed the aroma. Unfortunately she still couldn't discern any odors. Everything smelled the same.

"Did I add the chili powder, Dog?"

Dog wagged his tail.

She sighed and stirred some more. The soup looked

awfully bland. Chili was supposed to be spicy. Where was the measuring spoon? She didn't want to ruin her first meal for Mitch. She reached into the drawer, grabbed a serving spoon, and tried to taste the chili.

Her numb taste buds didn't offer any help.

She eyed the mixture one more time and decided to take a chance. She grabbed a clean measuring spoon from the drawer and poured the powder into its empty bowl.

This way she'd make sure it wasn't bland. Mitch deserved a good hot meal.

Mitch looked devastatingly handsome when he came to the table. He'd taken a shower and changed clothes. Instead of his blue denim, he wore a dark turtleneck.

"You look yummy." The words flew from her tongue.

He chuckled. "I think that's supposed to be my line."

"Why? Aren't women supposed to compliment men?"

He hooked his thumbs through the loops of his dark jeans and considered her question. "Everyone likes compliments." He took in her own creative attire.

"Aren't those the Halloween pants you found in the trunk?"

She grinned and pivoted. "What do you think?"

The blue of his eyes glinted. "I don't think that outfit ever looked so good."

Her insides went mushy under his warm glance.

"Are you ready to eat?" he asked.

She started. "Oops. I bet you're hungry."

"I am. Sorry, I'm late." He grabbed the salad bowl while she carried the bread basket to the table. "I had to call the vet. One of the cows had a run-in with the barbed wire."

"That sounds painful." Katerina loved the way the

## Yours FREE...
## when you reply today

This elegant necklace is classically styled with an exquisite heart pendant presented on a generous 46cm (18") silvertone chain. Respond today and it's all yours.

# YES. Please send me my two FREE books and welcome gift

PLACE
FREE GIFT
SEAL HERE

YES. I have placed my free gift seal in the space provided above. Please send me two free books and my welcome gift. I understand that I am under no obligation to purchase any books, as explained on the back and on the opposite page. I am over 18 years of age.

BLOCK CAPITALS                                                                    S1FI

Ms/Mrs/Miss/Mr                                          Initials

Surname

Address

                                                                    Postcode

*Thank you!*

No stamp needed.

# How The Silhouette® Reader Service™ works

Accepting free books and gifts places you under no obligation to buy anything. You may keep the books and gift and return the despatch note marked "cancel". If we don't hear from you, about a month later we will send you four new novels and invoice you for just £2.80* each. That's the complete price – there is no extra charge for postage and packing. You may cancel at any time, otherwise every month we'll send you four more books which you may purchase or return – the choice is yours.

*Terms and prices subject to change without notice.

SILHOUETTE READER SERVICE
FREE BOOK OFFER
FREEPOST CN81
CROYDON
CR9 3WZ

NO
STAMP
NEEDED

dim evening light brought out the rich tan of Mitch's skin.

"She'll be okay, but I'll have to have Toby repair that part of the fence."

Katerina scooted her chair forward. Her knees brushed Mitch's. The contact brought his gaze to her. Darn! She could feel a flush working its way up her neck.

"I hope you're hungry," she said brightly.

"Starved," he drawled.

She couldn't help herself. She peeked at him through her lashes. Mitch wasn't looking at his plate. His gaze devoured her instead.

"I found the napkins in the bureau with matching place mats." She was afraid she was going to start to babble if he didn't quit eating her with his eyes.

"They were a wedding gift."

Katerina hung on to her smile even though she felt a pierce of longing hit her midsection. Just for once, she'd like something to happen that didn't copy a page from the past.

She forced her regret aside and handed the soup tureen to Mitch.

Mitch ladled out a healthy portion. "I'm starving. I was ready to start eating a bale of hay, but I was afraid the herd would object."

"If I'd known you preferred a bale of hay, I could have cooked that instead."

His gaze glinted at her humor. "No, thanks. This will be fine."

She put her spoon to her mouth at the same time he tucked into his bowl.

"Aaugh!" Mitch coughed and grabbed his glass of water. He chugged down the entire glass. Then started coughing again.

"What's the matter?" She jumped to her feet and began to thump his back. Her heart pounded with fear. Tears were running down his face.

"What did you put in there?" he managed to gasp.

"Chili powder."

"How much?"

She tried to think back to preparing the meal. "The phone rang, and I lost track. I was worried it wouldn't have enough flavor."

"It's hot enough." He sounded as if his vocal chords had been fried. Tears streamed down his face. He blinked rapidly.

Katerina searched for something to help. She noticed his water glass was empty. She jumped to her feet and headed into the kitchen. Fortunately there was an ice-cold water pitcher in the refrigerator.

Mitch seemed to be breathing easier by the time she returned to the table. "I'm sorry. I should have been watching closer. They warned us about interruptions and the mistakes we could make if we weren't careful." She couldn't stop her nervous chatter of words. The twisted mass in her stomach wasn't about the food, but she didn't want to talk about what was really bothering her. "We'd have to write things down or keep a close eye on what we were doing. But I forgot about the phone. I should come up with a better system for handling recipes."

Mitch interrupted her, squeezing her fidgeting fingers. "Don't worry about it. Mistakes happen to all of us."

She was the one who had to blink back tears now. "Not like this. You're starving, and I've ruined dinner."

"I'll make a peanut butter sandwich. It's been the main staple of my diet for the past couple of months. I'll survive another meal or two." He gave her a crooked grin. "Do you want one, too?"

His willingness to overlook this calamity should have made her feel better. It didn't. "No, thanks. I've had enough. My taste buds don't mind what I put on them."

He looked ready to argue and then must have realized her taste buds weren't at all offended by the spicy food, since they didn't have the ability to know the difference.

He left the table and returned a few minutes later with a loaf of bread tucked under his arm and a jar of peanut butter.

He attacked his sandwiches, not seeming to mind his plain fare. She pushed aside her own plate. "I wanted to make you dinner as a way of thanking you."

"You don't need to thank me."

"You've been so kind and helpful. And you took me shopping and bought me wonderful clothes."

"You mean 'divine' clothes, don't you?" he said teasingly.

She tried to smile at his little joke, but she was too tense. She was determined to give her speech even though she'd made a mess of the meal that was supposed to be her gift. "I thought maybe I could give something back. You've lost so much. Your mother was never there. And then you lost your Katie. I thought this was the least I could do while I was here. But it didn't come out right."

Mitch set down the remainder of his sandwich and shoved aside his plate. "You don't owe me anything, Katie," he said flatly.

"Yes, I do. I ruined your dinner."

"You didn't ruin anything. Do you think this is the first time someone made a recipe that didn't turn out?"

"You act like this is an isolated incident, but it could be just the beginning of a nightmare for you." She waved her hand toward his half-eaten sandwich. "You're going to get tired of eating peanut butter sandwiches or trying to dilute overly spiced dishes. This isn't worth an ulcer.''

He frowned. "There are other foods, and I'm not picky.''

"I'm not talking about the chili,'' she snapped, frustrated with him and herself.

"Then what are we talking about?''

"Us.''

His gaze became hooded. "You want to move out because of an overdose of chili powder?''

He made it sound so trivial. "Of course not. I'm talking about expectations. This isn't what you wanted when you invited me to stay here. You have a busy life. You have a right to expect a good meal at the end of the day.''

"I didn't marry you to have a cook. If you want to, we can hire out.''

She jumped to her feet, her agitation making it impossible to sit still another moment. "That's ridiculous. You're being deliberately ridiculous.''

"Am I?'' He rose to his feet and placed his palms flat on the table to stare straight into her eyes. "It's no more ridiculous than saying a relationship doesn't work because of too much food spice.''

Katerina couldn't think when his eyes turned that intense shade of blue. They demanded a lot, and gave so little information in return.

"I need to be doing something. I feel useless and in the way.''

The firm line of his mouth strengthened. "You're not useless,'' he said with a deep huskiness that stroked and seduced in one breath. "Look at all you've accomplished in the space of a few months. Even the hospital administrator raved about the progress you made and how hard you worked. This isn't a setback. Life is full of dips and turns. We just learn to adjust.''

His tone softened. She almost relented until her gaze landed on the wedding picture sitting on the mantel behind him.

His logic wasn't about Katerina. He thought she was Katie. That's why he was giving her credit for things that weren't even virtues in her opinion. So what if she'd worked hard.

Yet, despite everything, Katerina had the insane urge to launch herself into his big strong arms and forget everything that stood between them. In the evening light, he appeared sexier and more attractive than a man should look.

His broad shoulders encased in a form-fitting turtleneck looked too inviting.

If only Katie didn't stand between them.

Katerina severed their eye connection and made her feet move to escape his magnetic pull before she lost the battle she was waging with herself.

She walked across the room and stared into her reflected image against the nighttime window. She rubbed her arms. ''Maybe we're trying to fool ourselves into making this work. We should consider the wisdom of ending this relationship before either of us gets hurt.''

''You said you'd stay for two months.''

She folded her arms tightly across her chest. ''Why should you put your life on hold until then?''

''I'm not putting my life on hold. Are you?''

''No.'' If only she were. Each day there was more of a danger for her here. She wanted things she couldn't have. Ever. Why couldn't he see what she saw? ''I'm different.''

"So you've never worn bright yellow before or come to dinner in Halloween pants. I can live with that."

"I thought you liked my new clothes."

"I love them." He closed the distance between them. She couldn't move back, even though she knew she should run in the opposite direction as fast as she could. When he was just a few steps away, he stopped and lifted a hand to her face. His touch, light and intimate, almost broke her heart. "You're not different. You're special."

For once she didn't want to talk. The emotions were welling up deep inside her. The back of her throat hurt from the suppression. "You'll end up hating me," she finally managed to whisper.

"For ruining chili?"

"For not being her. For not being your Katie."

He framed her face with his hands. His breath brushed her face and made her yearn for impossibilities. "Don't quit on me now, Katie."

"I'm trying to be practical."

"Why is it practical to run away without trying?" He asked the question almost quizzically. "Is that practical? Do you want to quit over a bowl of soup?"

"This isn't about soup."

"No, it's not." He put his hands on her shoulders and pulled her gently but firmly toward him. "You're running, Katie. Why?"

She should have resisted, but how did one push back Heaven?

She heard his heart beat and felt his breath on her cheek. Without thinking, she lifted her face toward his.

His lips descended slowly.

Running was the last thing she wanted to do.

The kiss should have been cool and foreign. It was

neither. It was warm and intimate. He seduced her with male tenderness. His whiskers tickled her skin, while his lips sipped and seduced.

She found herself pressed against his chest. In the distance she heard the pulsing of their hearts, so loud she could hear nothing else.

There was no awkwardness. Only familiarity and excitement. She wanted to be here as surely as if she'd followed a gilded path to the end of the rainbow.

Then his mouth opened against hers and her tongue sank into his. Heat spiraled through her pulse. She wrapped her fingers into his short tresses of hair.

''Katie,'' he murmured against her mouth.

She tried to close her ears. She didn't want to think about anything except how good his arms felt. Reality had never felt this good.

''God, I've missed you.'' His voice was so low, she might have missed what he was saying.

But in the back of her mind, a voice reminded her.

*Katie…he thinks you're his Katie. He wants you to be his Katie.*

Katerina made a superhuman effort to ignore the nagging reality. For a second she almost succeeded.

Almost.

She wrenched her mouth from his and ended the kiss. Resting her head against the powerful muscles of his chest, she heard the hammering of his heart and knew hers was pounding even more frantically.

She lifted her head. It was a mistake. The emotion she saw in his face nearly made her knees buckle. By its own willpower, her hand reached up to learn the hard edge of his jaw.

He reacted by turning his head ever so slightly and

pressing his mouth against the sensitive pulse in her wrist.

How could a man be soft and hard at the same time?

"You must have loved her very much," she whispered, unable to hold back her thoughts.

"I love *you* very much," he corrected her.

She shook her head, knowing and fearing the real truth he wouldn't admit. She didn't want to believe his statement made a difference. But it made all the difference in the world.

How could she know if this kiss was meant for her, or for the woman he married? He didn't know the difference.

Yet, she knew deep inside of her there was a big one.

There had always been this peril. She'd known it even in the hospital. The intimate pull between them had been there almost from the moment she'd first awakened. Now she knew the real truth. Love was the biggest danger. How easy it would be to fall in love with Mitch. How incredibly wonderful. How perilous.

Mitch was the sexiest man she remembered meeting. Even the detectives didn't have an ounce of his magnetism. She knew the minute Mitch entered the room, and when he left. She could watch him for hours striding through the barnyard, herding cattle in the pasture, or hefting feed bags from the back of his pickup. His strength and sure-handedness sported its own brand of high-level intoxication.

She wanted him.

He belonged to another woman.

How could there be any hope for a possible future when he loved another woman? Another woman with Katerina's face.

She was playing with fire if she denied the reality. She might survive a bump on the head, but she wouldn't survive loving and ultimately losing Mitch.

That knowledge reverberated through her soul.

Self-preservation came to her stead and fortified her waning courage.

With great reluctance, Katerina pushed against his muscled chest.

Mitch resisted for only a moment. Then his arms gave way.

Praying her wobbly knees would support her, she stepped back, unable to meet his compelling gaze. "I'm sorry," she said. "That shouldn't have happened."

"Shouldn't it?" His mouth turned up, but there was no humor in his grin. "Maybe that's exactly what we should be doing."

She braved his derision. "Can you honestly say you weren't thinking about Katie?"

He released an impatient sigh.

"There isn't a difference. You're one and the same."

"No, we're not. And we never will be."

She didn't wait for him to respond. She left the table of dirty dishes and escaped to her bedroom.

Leaning against the doorway, she squeezed her eyes closed and relived the kiss. Of anything she was bound to forget, she knew she wouldn't be able to erase that from her mind. The heat of his mouth lingered on her lips.

How ironic she couldn't discern the flavor of a potent kitchen spice, but the taste of Mitch was stamped into her senses.

If she wanted to, she couldn't forget him.

Ironically, she'd found a powerful antidote for curing

short-term memory loss. If she was smart, she'd find a way to patent it and sell it on the open market.

But at what price?

She already feared he owned her heart, whether he truly wanted it or not.

# *Chapter 8*

Mitch didn't move for five minutes after Katie left the room. If he had, he would have marched down the hall and knocked down the door that separated them.

Hell, he hadn't expected this to be easy. But to have his wife back in his arms, only to have her leave them again was worse than the abstinence of the past few months.

Ironically, it hadn't been his passion that had scared her off.

She'd responded to him with an innocence and enthusiasm more powerful than any potent aphrodisiac.

She'd pulled away because he wasn't willing to pretend she wasn't who she was.

He shook his head. What was he supposed to do?

Forget what they'd meant to each other?

Forget the dreams?

The promises?

The temptation to do just that battled his own sense of

integrity. Would it be so bad to give her the words she needed to hear? Eventually she'd come to understand that the past was not the enemy. Wouldn't she?

They could rekindle and make right what had gone wrong.

Clancy nudged his arm. The dog hadn't followed her into the bedroom. But he didn't look happy about being left with Mitch.

The dog gave him a questioning look.

Mitch had no answers. He could no more pretend that the world was flat than pretend his marriage to Katie hadn't counted. It was the only thing that had mattered. Even making this farm a success didn't measure an inch compared to his relationship to the woman behind the closed door.

It was as if she were half a world away.

He started to gather the dirty dishes, throwing out the half-eaten sandwich. His appetite for food had evaporated.

His immediate hunger would be harder to assuage.

The dog kept pace next to him. When Mitch finished stacking the dishwasher, he started the machine.

"Come on, Clancy. Let's check out the livestock. We can keep each other company."

Clancy didn't argue, but he didn't wag his tail with great joy, either.

"Don't feel bad, boy." Mitch grabbed his coat. "We're in this together. Cows aren't my first choice of companionship, either."

Katerina looked through the viewfinder of the small camera and pressed the zoom button to adjust the lens. The late-afternoon light gave the room a rosy hue, high-lighting different corners. She focused on the plant sitting next to the floor lamp. Mastering the little machine had become her primary focus over the past few days. It gave her something to do.

Mitch was avoiding her. Since the kiss, he'd made excuses to not spend a lot of time in the house.

This was a busy time of year with the livestock. Calves were arriving every day. Mitch had explained he preferred this time of year to breed because of the weather. He could use the outside maternity pens instead of the interior stalls that had to be covered with a thick rubber mat, a lime compound and straw. Mitch was keeping a close eye on certain cows that had had difficulty in the past with their deliveries as well as the heifers who were experiencing their first pregnancies. Mitch had three farmhands to take some of the responsibility, but she'd overheard him on the phone giving one of the hands some unexpected time off.

He was definitely avoiding spending time alone with her.

Katerina didn't blame him for keeping his distance. They both needed some breathing space. But while he had a job, she didn't have anything to occupy her time.

When she could drive again, she'd have more power over her time. She'd already spoken to Toby about giving her some driving lessons.

She prepared dinner last night with greater success. The phone hadn't rung, and she managed to keep the ingredients straight. Mitch had been complimentary and polite.

The strain between them had been taxing. She wouldn't have believed it possible to have an aching jaw, but that's exactly what she'd endured by keeping up an endless stream of chatter. Mitch had excused himself and left the house as soon as he'd finished. She'd been left to converse with Dog.

Unfortunately she still hadn't decoded the dog's tail-wagging language. Maybe it was something she could suggest to the doctor at her next appointment. The convalescent home should offer a course on translating wagging tails.

"Do you want to pose for me?" she asked her faithful companion.

Dog sat back on his haunches and panted.

She adjusted, zoomed and clicked. Lowering the camera, she walked over and rubbed the dog's furry chin. "You're a great model. Anytime you need a reference, I'll be happy to furnish one."

The dog's tail thumped noisily against the wood floor. She interpreted that to mean he was grateful.

Before she could find another subject to target, the phone rang.

Katerina grabbed it before its second ring. She didn't care who it was; at least she'd have someone human to talk to.

"Katie, this is Mandy from the Bakerstown Police Department."

Katerina remembered the woman detective. "Hello, Mandy."

"How have you been doing?"

Katerina had an inkling the question wasn't idle curiosity. "I'm feeling stronger each day. But if you're asking me if I remember anything more about my job, then the answer is no."

The detective sighed heavily into the phone. "I was afraid of that, but I had to ask."

"Has something happened?"

Before she could answer, the dog barked and raced to the door.

Craning her neck, Katerina peered out the window and saw a strange car in the driveway. "Someone just drove into the yard," she said into the phone.

"If it's a tan car, it's probably Rafe."

"Rafe?" The name sounded familiar.

"My partner. He said he might stop by. He can fill you in. I'll catch you later." The detective hung up before Katerina could say goodbye.

The other detective didn't come to the house right away. Grasping the dog's collar, Katerina opened the door to see where her visitor was. The big man stood next to his car, talking to Mitch.

The two men didn't notice her watching them. Whatever they were discussing dominated their attention.

Dog whined.

Katerina sympathized with the canine. She opened the door wider and called, "Are you both going to stand out there or are you coming in?"

The men turned toward her.

Mitch's expression was terse and guarded.

Rafe gave her a big, loopy grin. "Hi, Katie."

He strode forward, with Mitch slowly following.

"You're a sight for sore eyes." Rafe gave her a quick hug. "The department hasn't been the same without you."

She searched his face and then Mitch's as they came into the house. "Something's wrong, isn't it?"

At first neither of the men answered her.

"Tell me," she demanded.

Mitch tossed his hat onto the table. "There's been a development in the case with the little boy."

"Jacob?"

Rafe nodded. "Someone attempted to snatch him from his grandmother's front yard."

She released the dog's collar. "Was Jacob hurt? Is he okay?"

"He's a smart kid. He managed to bite the guy's hand and take off. We've got him at the police station."

"What are you going to do? He should be protected. He's just a little boy."

"We want to put him and his grandmother in protective custody, but Mrs. Peterson refuses to go. Her other daughter is due to have a baby any day, and she's promised to be there for the delivery. She's torn between Jacob and her daughter."

"Can Jacob go with her?"

Rafe hesitated. "The daughter lives in Jasonville, just fifteen minutes away. It wouldn't be hard for someone to track them down. She and her husband are listed in the phone book. Mrs. Peterson doesn't know what to do. Since this guy is getting bolder in his attempts to snatch the boy and Jacob has a penchant for slipping out of his grandmother's sight, she's afraid she'll lose him, too. She's already lost her daughter. At the same time, she doesn't want the boy to be too far away from her."

"Where will he go if you put him in protective custody?"

"We're working on something. But the kid's been so traumatized, we can't just assign him to anyone. Since he responds to you…"

"I'll stay with him," Katerina interrupted. "You can put us in a hotel or something. I'll keep him safe. Just let me put a few things together."

Mitch grabbed her arm as she came abreast of him. "Wait. I think we can come up with a better solution."

As upset as she was, she didn't pull away from him.

She saw the concern in his blue eyes. "He shouldn't be with strangers," she insisted adamantly.

Mitch shook his head. "He won't be if he comes here."

"Here?" Her resistance fled. He seemed absolutely sincere.

Rafe frowned. "I'm not trying to foist the kid on you."

"You're not." There was no hesitation in Mitch's voice. "Having him here would be the perfect answer all the way around. The kid trusts Katie, and no one will look for him here."

Rafe nodded, a bit of relief lightening the stern edges of his face. "Yeah, that might be the solution. Let me call and check with the captain."

While Rafe was on the phone, Katerina plucked Mitch's sleeve. "Thank you," she said to him. "We'll keep him safe."

"You don't have to thank me. I wouldn't sleep nights if I thought that little guy was in danger."

A tremulous smile came to her face. "You're going to make a great father someday," she said, the words tumbling out of her mouth.

Mitch looked stunned by her out-of-the-blue comment. "What makes you say that?" he asked, his voice husky.

"Because you know what it's like to be alone, and you'll never allow your child to live with that emptiness."

"And what about you?"

"What kind of parent will I be?" She had trouble seeing herself objectively. "I guess I just want to be the kind of parent who keeps trying, even when I make mistakes."

Before Mitch could respond, Rafe ended his call and rejoined them. "Captain Loomis is all for it. He'll talk to the grandmother. We'll give you a call about the arrangements.''

"Maybe we should come with you to get Jacob," Katerina suggested, needing to see for herself that the child was okay.

"No, it'll be better if we bring him to you. We want to keep his location a secret. We'll sneak him out of the building so no one can associate his sudden disappearance with either of you."

Mitch accompanied Rafe to his car.

"We appreciate this," Rafe told him as he climbed into his unmarked car.

Mitch nodded. "It'll give Katie something to do during the day. She's getting a little bored."

"I'll bet."

"The doctor has given her permission to start driving."

"You don't sound too thrilled."

Mitch hadn't meant to spill his guts. "I'm just not ready to have her out of my sight."

Rafe nodded and gave him a quick salute before pulling out of the driveway.

Mitch watched the car leave and then headed toward the barn. He still didn't trust himself in the house alone with Katie. Especially since she'd be excited and grateful—potent ingredients that could ignite a combustible situation. If he didn't want that very thing, he'd throw caution to the winds.

But his resistance to Katie was at an all-time low. He wanted her with every fiber of his being. He wasn't nearly as worried about her job these days as he was about what would happen if he let down his guard around her. Being in the house with her provided ripe breeding grounds for seduction. She'd stroke him with one of those butterfly touches of hers and he'd go up in flames.

At night he couldn't close his eyes without envisioning how many footsteps were between her bed and his. The worst part was, she didn't sleep much herself. He knew that she roamed the house late at night and peeked into his room several times. It was all he could do not to reach out and pull her into bed with him. Her image in the doorway, long after she drifted away, taunted him. She'd taken to wearing one of his old shirts. The long tails barely came to her mid thighs. He didn't think there was anything sexier than a woman wearing a man's shirt. It symbolized a bond and a connection.

Just thinking about the what-ifs made Mitch's blood heat. He needed a physical release.

Striding into the barn, he grabbed the pitchfork and drove it into a bale of hay. He commanded his mind to think about the logistics of Jacob's arrival.

The child's presence would be a welcome diversion for both him and Katie. Maybe they'd all get some sleep.

Hell, the state his body was in, he wouldn't count on it.

Jacob arrived two hours later in a nondescript car. This time Mandy made the trip, but she was dressed in a baggy pant outfit that thoroughly camouflaged her identity. She looked like an aging teenager.

The little boy didn't say anything when Katerina came out to greet him, but his face lit into a wide smile. He carried a tattered brown bear.

Mandy delivered his suitcase to the house and left while Katerina gave Jacob a tour of his new home.

"Would you and Mr. Bear like to sleep in this bed in my room?"

The boy timidly walked into the room and looked around. He glanced at the big bed and then at the smaller one.

"Yes, this is my bed." Katerina bounced on the big bed.

Jacob moved over to the cot and placed his raggedy bear on the pillow. Then he, too, made a playful bounce as if to stake his claim to that space.

Katerina wanted to gather the lost soul in her arms, but she knew she needed to wait until he was ready to be hugged. He'd gone through so much in the past few months. She wanted him to feel secure in his new surroundings and with her. It couldn't be forced.

She heard Mitch come into the house and the familiar clicking of Clancy's nails as they crossed the wood floors.

The moment Mitch arrived, Jacob's eyes widened with apprehension. He slipped from the bed and moved close to Katerina.

"It's okay. This is Mitch. Do you remember him?"

Jacob nodded.

Katerina noticed Jacob wasn't watching Mitch. His gaze had fastened on the golden-furred dog.

Mitch kept his hand locked around the straining dog's collar. "Clancy, sit," she said. She'd finally committed the dog's name to memory.

The dog sat.

"Okay, shake Jacob's hand, so he knows you're his friend."

The dog put up his paw.

The boy watched in fascination. He cocked his head questioningly toward Katerina.

She smiled. "Clancy wants to be friends. He likes to

play and—'' she whispered into his ear ''—he likes ice cream.''

The corners of Jacob's mouth lifted. He cautiously approached the dog. Katerina came with him. She shook the paw first. "Good dog, Clancy."

Jacob bravely stuck his own hand out and clasped the dog's limb.

Suddenly Clancy leaned over and licked the boy's face.

Jacob shrugged his shoulders and giggled. Then he bravely reached over and petted the furry animal's thick coat.

Mitch released the collar, but stayed close so the dog wouldn't jump and overwhelm his new friend. He need not have worried. The boy and dog formed an instant rapport.

Wherever Jacob went, the dog followed.

Katerina wasn't surprised, but she was bemused by Mitch's reaction. Instead of fleeing out of the house as had been his practice the past few days, he stayed inside.

Katerina went into the bedroom and unpacked Jacob's suitcase, while Mitch brought out Clancy's rope. She returned to find the two males involved in a game of tug-of-war with the canine. Watching them roll around the floor, she was struck by the simple normalcy of the scene. No one would ever know that this wasn't a real family. The lightness on Mitch's face was an expression she'd never seen before. She had the amazing need to capture it so she could remember.

She picked up the camera she'd left sitting on the end table.

Her first attempt to snap a photo didn't work. She forgot how to turn on the flash. It took a few minutes to pinpoint which button she should push.

She finally figured out she had to press the button marked with a squiggly bolt. She tried again and met with success.

The flash brought the attention of both males.

Lowering the camera, she met Mitch's gaze. Within the twin blue lights, she witnessed a strong need and something else, as well.

Desire?

Katerina's breath caught in the back of her throat. She didn't want to hope. Ever since she'd awaken from the coma, she'd had a niggling feeling that something was missing. It wasn't just the pieces of her past that bothered her. She had a deep hunger that she wanted more from life.

She'd thought it might be a job. She wanted something to fulfill her. But combing through the want ads and visiting the police department hadn't scratched the itch entirely.

Now she looked at Jacob giggling at the dog. She saw the way he returned again and again to Mitch's lap, seeking his attention and approval.

What was she seeing? What was tugging at her heart?

A child's trust? The budding of bond between the man and child?

Katerina clutched the camera tightly. A blinding flash echoed through the room.

"I think you just took a picture of the floor," Mitch drawled, a hint of teasing laughter coloring his tone.

An odious tear slid down her face. She dashed away the unwanted wetness with the back of her hand. "Oh, good. We didn't have a picture of the floor yet. Now you'll have one."

Jacob giggled.

Mitch tugged on the boy's ear. "Isn't she a smart woman, Jacob?"

The little boy looked from one to the other as if he didn't quite understand this grown-up silly talk. He gave them both a wide grin.

Just then the phone shrilled.

Since Mitch had Jacob on his lap, Katerina reached for it. "Hello?"

There was no answering salutation on the other end.

"Hello?" she tried again.

From across the room, Mitch and Jacob watched her. She saw Jacob shrink closer to Mitch.

She replaced the receiver.

"No one there?" Mitch asked without emotion.

Katerina met his dark gaze. "It must have been a wrong number."

Mitch's hands settled reassuringly around Jacob's shoulders. "Yeah, I'm sure someone just made a mistake."

Katerina wondered if she'd just imagined the breathing she thought she'd heard at the other end of the phone line.

The phone rang again. This time Mitch grabbed the receiver, but kept Jacob anchored close to him.

"Hello?"

His demeanor relaxed. "Hello, Mrs. Peterson. Yes, Jacob is sitting right here."

Katerina's tension eased.

As Mitch let Jacob listen to his grandmother speak, Katerina straightened the room and put away the dog's toys. She was conscious of Mitch's gaze following her.

She'd thought Jacob's arrival would make things easier for them. They'd have someone to ease the electrical awareness that energized the room whenever they were both in it.

But the boy's presence seemed to act as a stronger conduit. She couldn't keep the barriers up between them. Her heart beat faster. Her skin tingled. And inside, she felt like mush. She wanted to hold this child close and be held in return by Mitch's big strong arms. The ache spiraled from the tips of her toes to the center of her body. She didn't know what she felt. Or why she wanted the feeling to be much more than an intangible longing.

After the phone call Mitch asked Jacob, "How would you like a dish of ice cream before you get ready for bed?"

The boy stood and started toward the kitchen.

"I guess that means yes." Mitch winked at Katerina before rising to his feet.

"I guess it does." She hoped he couldn't hear her heart hammering inside her chest. She didn't follow them to the kitchen.

With Clancy eagerly leading the way to the ice cream, Jacob slipped his small hand into Mitch's.

The glimmer of eagerness on the child's face revealed a solid case of hero worship.

Katerina understood the feeling too well.

It would be so easy to fall for Mitch. He had the strength and steadiness a traumatized child needed to enjoy life again.

Hadn't that been part of the reason she'd decided to stay here? She'd needed his surety and comfort when the world had been strange and out of focus.

But now she wondered if there wasn't a bigger danger.

She feared she was falling in love with a man who couldn't see her for herself, and she didn't know how to stop herself from the sure free fall.

## *Chapter 9*

Mitch decided it would be best to escape the house while Katie put Jacob to bed. The charged atmosphere between him and Katie had heightened to an all-time high. By the time Jacob finished his ice cream, they were avoiding each other's eyes.

Mitch welcomed the bracing spring air against his face, even though Katie's womanly scent followed him out of the house.

That hadn't changed since the day they'd met.

Mitch pulled open the barn door and stepped inside. The musty aroma of fresh straw filled his nostrils. He shook his head. The image of Katie, in her colorful wrap skirt, and how she'd looked bending over Jacob as they walked to the bedroom, stood front and center in his mind. She had an intuitive maternalness with the child. She didn't hide behind an emotional barricade as she did with Mitch. She bestowed hugs and kisses freely, not having to rein in the touchy-feely side of her. The small boy wasn't stupid; he greedily basked in the warmth, and Mitch didn't blame him. He'd give his entire acreage for all that touching and feeling she generously bestowed.

Mitch brought himself up short and realized he'd been standing in the doorway daydreaming. Even a barn full of cows couldn't erase the woman.

He wanted to check on two new calves that had been born earlier in the day. One of the calves, which hadn't presented itself correctly until Mitch had taken a hand, hadn't been able to stand. While Mitch wasn't overly concerned, he needed to make sure he was progressing.

Walking deeper into the barn, the sounds of the live-stock greeted him. He found the mother cow hunkered down in the hay, chewing her cud. The two calves rested nearby. One of them tried to climb to his wobbly feet and greet him as he moved into the stall.

"Hi, fella." He pushed the calf over to his mother.

The calf bleated and sank to his knees before lying down next to his twin. The twin struggled but couldn't stand.

"Need a little help?" he asked the calf while he examined her. The calf was stronger than when Mitch had checked her before. He gently lifted her and helped her stand on her shaky legs.

The calf ma-a-aed loudly, but didn't collapse. Her twin stood again and nuzzled her dark brown look-alike.

They'd both be okay.

Watching them, Mitch wished he had that kind of assurance. He was in sorrier shape now than he'd been before Jacob had arrived. He wanted Katie more now than ever, and there wasn't a thing he could do about it.

Mitch straightened and backed out of the stall, closing the gate behind him.

Damn, holding himself in check was harder than wrestling with an ornery bull. Those bright clothes she wore sent his libido into overdrive. He wanted things to be real and natural between them. He sensed that part of her wanted that, too.

After she'd given Jacob a big hug, she'd started to reach for Mitch and caught herself. She hadn't said anything, but the wisp of pink covering her cheeks told the story.

Mitch hadn't been able to move. He wanted that embrace. He still did. His senses were steeped in the essence of Katie. No matter what he did or where he did it, he carried her with him.

But if he was truthful, he'd realize that part of him dreaded it, too.

She hadn't talked about leaving, but he knew she would. His mother had been emotionally absent. And Katie herself had pushed him away in their marriage.

Why?

Was he to blame? Was there something unlovable about him?

He didn't know. Was that his fear? Tonight he'd seen something in Katie's eyes. He hadn't known how to identify it at first. The softness around her mouth. The intriguing glint in her green eyes. She seemed happy. Content. Her hair took on a life of its own in the reddish sheen of the evening light. He wanted to bury his face in the heavy thickness. He might have followed through on his impulses until he realized what he was witnessing. The picture in front of him was every fantasy he'd ever envisioned. A wife. A child. A happy home. They were the threads he'd tried to weave through his marriage.

But something had always been missing.

He sensed there was something still out of sync that had nothing to do with Katie's memory loss.

He wasn't anchored in the past. Nothing bored him more than harping on old adventures. He was a man of the future, who always looked ahead. That's how he'd survived his lonely childhood. He created his reality and applied all of his resources to making it happen. Control had been the device he'd used to make everything go his way.

Yet, from the moment he'd met Katie he'd had no control. The more he'd tried to control her, the more she'd resisted. And in the end, she'd left. He could honestly admit that the best times had been when he'd taken the greatest risk and had no control.

And that's what would happen again. Unfortunately, losing control scared the hell out of him more now than it ever had. Now he knew how it felt to lose the most important being on this earth. How could he risk that?

He didn't want to live within the realm of fear. His wife didn't remember him, and the child would be here for only a few days. Mitch knew he couldn't get too comfortable in this role.

But he wanted more than anything for these few days to last forever. When his world could be just the way he wanted it.

Jacob's lack of speech didn't present any handicap to his enjoyment of the farm. He got up bright and early to help feed the cows. When Mitch brought him into the house, there wasn't an ounce of him that wasn't caked in mud.

"Jacob tried to make a castle in the manure pile."

Katerina laughed. "Come on, fella. Let's clean you before you eat your breakfast."

Jacob had just as much fun in the bathtub as he did in the barnyard. He dived beneath the bubbles that Katerina had added to his water, made the soap dish into a boat, and used his hands to torpedo it.

After she coaxed him out of the tub, he tucked into the French toast Mitch had prepared.

"What are you two going to do today?" Mitch asked.

"I thought we'd take some pictures of the farm so Jacob can have something to show to his grandmother when he goes home," Katerina said.

Jacob's eyes lit up. His head tilted in a question.

"Yes, you can take some of the pictures," she answered as if he'd articulated the words with his voice.

He grinned and started to leave the table.

Katerina stopped him. "Whoops, come back here. We've got to help clean up the table first."

He sped back to the table and picked up his plate. Mitch showed him where to put the utensils in the dishwasher before he left the house to resume his chores.

After Katerina and Jacob finished cleaning up the kitchen, she pulled their coats from the closet. They were almost to the door when the phone rang.

Katerina lifted the receiver. "Hello?"

Silence reigned at the other end.

She felt the familiar uneasiness tap jarringly on her nerves.

Jacob suddenly launched himself at her leg and hung on tight. Looking down, she saw fear dilate his pupils.

She replaced the phone carefully. Then she used her body to shield the offensive instrument from Jacob's view. "Are you ready to take my picture?" She offered the shiny-faced camera to the boy.

Her strategy worked. He unlatched his grip and cradled the camera gently in his hands.

Clancy bounded out the door with them, and whatever

fear Jacob showed in the house disappeared in the bright
morning light.

Katerina vowed she'd do everything in her power to
keep it that way.


Jacob fell asleep on the sofa immediately after lunch.

Katerina wasn't in the least tired. She kept thinking
about the phone calls. Another call had come just after
they arrived back at the house.

She heard Mitch clean up in the mudroom before he
entered the room in his stocking feet. He saw the sleeping
boy nestled at her side. "Should I carry him to bed?"
Mitch asked in a low voice.

She shook her head. "No, let him nap here. I can keep
a closer eye on him."

Her worry must have translated itself to Mitch. "Is
something wrong?" he asked tersely.

She absently pressed her hand to her scar. "I don't
know." She lowered her voice so she wouldn't disturb
Jacob. "We got two more mystery phone calls this morning."

"Mystery phone calls?"

She searched for the right words. "I don't know how
to explain them. The phone rings, but no one is there.
Yet…" Her voice trailed off.

"There's something odd about the calls?"

"I have this feeling that there's someone waiting on
the other end."

"Waiting for what?"

"I don't know. I know it sounds dumb, but you don't
suppose this has something to do with Jacob and his
mother's accident, do you? No one knows he's here,
right?"

"I don't know." Mitch couldn't be sure of anything.

Mandy and Rafe had taken extra pains to make sure no one knew where Jacob was going. Only a few people knew the child was here. In this case, a few people could be one too many.

Katie slipped carefully away from Jacob and stood. She paced the width of the floor, because she couldn't stand still.

Mitch couldn't take his eyes from her. She'd chosen to wear the orange jumpsuit. On anyone else it would have looked absurdly flamboyant. On Katie, it was sex personified.

She stopped in front of him and hooked her hand through the crook of his arm. Mitch sucked in a sharp breath. He should be used to her impulsive touches by now.

Could one get used to lightning?

Not unless he was dead. And Mitch certainly wasn't dead.

"Call Mandy at the department," he suggested. "It won't hurt for them to take more precautions. Or us, either."

Her gaze widened. "What precautions should we take?"

"Don't leave the house without Clancy," he said tersely. Hopefully she'd think his terseness stemmed from his concern for the child and not because he had a lock over his burning loins. "And don't answer the phone unless I'm here. If it's Jacob's grandmother or someone else we know, they'll leave a message, and you can call back."

He waited to see if she'd argue. She didn't.

By the time he left the room, she was talking on the phone to the detective.

Clancy didn't move from her side.

*  *  *

Mitch spent an hour doing research on the Internet. He intended to go to a cattle auction in a few weeks and wanted to see what would be available.

After he shut down his computer, he strode to the machine shed to find Ben, his hired hand. They worked together to tune up the old Jeep.

Ben was the big, silent-type, except when it came to the Packers. Then he never ran out of words. That suited Mitch fine, since the other man's four letter adjectives about the Packers's most recent trade was a daily litany and helped steer Mitch's mind away from Katie.

They were almost finished when the door opened. Mitch pulled his head out from under the hood and spotted Katie and Jacob coming toward him.

"Jacob wants to take your picture," Katie said. "Yours, too, Ben."

Ben nearly bumped his head on the hood at the sound of her voice. The older man gave Mitch a trapped look. Mitch wasn't sure if his shock stemmed from Katie's iridescent orange attire, or her planting herself between them so Jacob could flash a photo.

"Press the gray button when you've got us lined up," she coached the boy.

As she gestured, her body twisted so that her derriere lined up snug against Mitch's front.

Mitch gritted his teeth. From the corner of his eye, he saw Ben give him a blank look. Hell, was there anything worse than getting turned on in the middle of the day, under a camera's glare? He hoped Jacob didn't aim the camera too low.

The camera flashed.

Katie clapped her hands and leaned toward the little boy. "That's great."

Then she turned around. "Jacob wants to know if we can take a picture of all three of you?"

Mitch wondered how she knew what the small boy was thinking when he hadn't said a word.

Whether she was right or wrong, the boy came forward and moved in between the two men. Ben shifted nervously until after the bulb went off.

"Are we done here?" the older man said gruffly.

Mitch gave him a sympathetic grin. "That should do it for today. Why don't you go out and check the fence on the east side of the pasture?"

Relief swamped Ben's face. He tipped his head toward Katie and excused himself.

"I think we made him nervous." Katie's green eyes were alight with laughter.

"Can you blame him? I don't think he's ever seen that color of orange before."

"Really?" She looked down at her attire. "Does he prefer another color?"

Mitch couldn't hold back a grin. "Why don't you ask him the next time you see him?"

She gave him a sly look. "I just might do that."

If he'd had any doubt before, he knew now that she was deliberately teasing him.

Mitch felt a tug at his midsection. What kind of game was she playing? He had a feeling that she'd purposefully staged this scene. She knew exactly the havoc she was creating when she nestled her tight behind against the front of his jeans.

Whatever Katie was up to, he had neither the stamina nor the desire to resist. This risk he was willing to take.

# Chapter 10

Gazing up at the sight above her, Katerina didn't think there was anything sexier than a man with a tear in his jeans, dangling from a tree, cursing a stubborn branch.

"Da—darn it, Katie, do you think you could get me a ladder before I fall and break my neck?" Mitch growled.

"I could try and catch you."

Mitch's gaze narrowed to thin slats. "You're getting quite a chuckle out of this, aren't you?"

"Almost as much as the one you got when I was trying to throw a ball to your dog." She fiddled with the camera and then snapped a photo.

"You're quite brassy, knowing that I can't reach your scrawny neck."

"Scrawny? Is that what you really think?" She was having too much fun at his expense. It was nice to be the one with the superior hand for a change.

He sighed. "I don't think your neck is scrawny or anything else. Now will you get the ladder?"

Jacob, who hadn't been able to stand still while Mitch hung the swing, had been throwing sticks for Clancy to catch. Now he came to her side. He pointed to Mitch.

Katerina might be able to withstand Mitch's bossy order, but she couldn't ignore the wistful plea in Jacob's big brown eyes.

She grabbed the ladder and pushed it against the tree trunk.

Mitch didn't waste any time getting out of his scratchy perch. He jumped the last few steps.

He stood back to admire his handiwork. "What do you think?"

Katerina critically surveyed it. "I guess it will do."

Mitch folded his arms. "It'll do, all right."

Jacob pranced around them in excitement. At Clancy's bark, the boy picked up another stick and threw it a good fifteen feet.

"Nice throw," Mitch commented. Then a wicked gleam crept into his eyes. "You've already got Katie beat by a mile."

Katerina gave him her nastiest glare. "I should have left you in the tree."

He leaned over and mussed her hair. "You're cute when you get all riled up."

The warm feeling of pleasure swirling through her brought a smile to her lips. "You're not so bad yourself."

Mitch gave her a slow wink before turning to the little boy. "Are you ready to test this yet, Jacob?"

He didn't have to ask the child twice.

The boy climbed into the circular tube and pulled up his feet so Mitch could push him. Within minutes, the boy was sailing high over the yard in the tire.

When Mitch got called away to tend to a crisis in the

barn, Katerina took over as the chief pusher. She managed to snap a few pictures to add to her collection.

After half an hour in the swing, she coaxed Jacob into scavenging the farmyard for more subjects to photograph. They made their way to the barn and found Toby and Mitch loading a wagon of bales to be transported to the feedlot.

Katerina's breath caught at the sensual image Mitch made. He'd slipped off his jacket and unbuttoned the top clasps of his denim shirt. The sheen of perspiration brought out the dark skin tone of his throat. Katerina felt her breath trap in her lungs. Damn, the man looked sexy no matter what he did.

He looked up and caught her staring.

She reached for her camera and hid her embarrassment behind the lens. Without counting, she snapped frame after frame.

Mitch reached down and pulled Jacob up beside him on the flatbed. The boy sat on the stack of bales as Mitch and Toby worked.

Jacob didn't want to leave the men after they finished their chores, so they followed them to the machine shed. Katerina filled a complete roll of film with shots of the boy riding Mitch's shoulders as they crossed the farmyard.

A deep longing tweaked Katerina's heartstrings. Mitch was a serious, driven man. Yet he knew how to play and nurture. It would be so easy to fall in love with Mitch.

Would it hurt to just pretend a little? To taste the forbidden?

Why shouldn't she compete with Katie for Mitch?

He wanted her.

She wanted him.

It wasn't as though the other Katie was going to pop up again. That woman no longer existed.

Katerina was ready to step up to the plate and take her chances.

What could it hurt? She couldn't be in any more misery than she'd been before. Even if this was just pretend, she wanted to try.

The next morning Katerina and Jacob hiked the bluff overlooking the river. She was amazed at the boy's contentment. There was no question he felt safe at the farm. He no longer jumped at the sound of the phone ringing, even though they were still receiving mystery calls.

His grandmother called every night and spoke to him before he went to bed. Jacob settled right down to sleep after he heard his grandmother's voice.

Katerina sat on the blanket she'd brought along and watched Jacob play with Clancy. Jacob looked happy and content. The only thing abnormal was his inability to talk. Whatever terrible thing he'd witnessed at the time of his mother's death, it had caused him to shut down his vocal cords. Other than that, he was a perfectly normal little boy.

Jacob rolled down the hillside while Clancy barked and gave chase.

The two were already great pals. It seemed that Clancy had made Jacob forget to be afraid.

Unfortunately for Katerina, a dog's affection couldn't solve her affliction. She had a gnawing feeling that only Mitch would do that.

She, too, wanted to hide from a past she couldn't remember. Whatever happened between her and Mitch was still between them. The good and the bad. It would be so much easier if she could forever erase those years from

everyone else's memory, too. But she didn't have that
option.

If only Mitch weren't so attractive, so manly. He
seemed to have become an intense part of her life, even
though it would be better if she could let him go.

She didn't want another woman's husband. She didn't
want to be compared to another woman.

If she walked away for good, would she ever be able
to forget him?

No. Not this time.

The questions whirling through her head didn't have
answers. The best solution was to address them to Mitch.
Only he could tell her the answers.

But Katerina wasn't sure she was ready for that kind
of confrontation. She deliberately forced her thoughts
away from her topsy-turvy life.

From her vantage point, she could look over Mitch's
vast property. The day basked in the spring sunshine. The
trees were already starting to bud. It wouldn't be long
before the landscape was full and lush. There was a
strong feeling of renewal in the air. She heard a calf bleat,
and his mother's answering call. To her left she saw the
herd of brown cows grazing on the pasture.

From the corner of her eye, she saw a car approach
the lane of Mitch's driveway. It slowed, but didn't turn
in.

The car wasn't familiar. She put the camera to her eye
and tried to bring the car into focus through the zoom
lens. The car was too far away for her to get a good shot.
She took only one picture.

The car stopped. It suddenly occurred to her how vulnerable they were, sitting out in the open.

She gathered up her blanket. ''Jacob, why don't we go
down and see if Mitch is home yet?''

An expression of uncertainty crossed the child's face. But at the mention of Mitch's name, he nodded.

The car was long gone by the time they reached the house, but Katerina didn't want to take any chances. She ushered Jacob inside the house.

She was making him a peanut butter sandwich when Mitch strode into the house.

"How are you doing, little man?" Mitch asked, ruffling the youngster's hair.

Jacob gave him a big grin, revealing a mouthful of peanut butter.

Mitch placed a package on the table. "Here's your pictures and a couple more rolls of film."

"You got them developed already?"

Katerina immediately forgot what she was doing and reached for the package.

The teakettle on the stove shrieked.

Mitch intercepted the noisemaker, setting it off to the side. "What do you need the hot water for?"

Hot water? She tried to think. "I'm not sure."

Jacob slipped from his chair, ran to the counter, and handed Katerina a package of Jell-O.

She smiled. "Thanks, sweetheart. We were making strawberry Jell-O. How could I forget?"

Jacob climbed back onto his stool and grabbed his sandwich.

Mitch saw him give half of his portion to Clancy, who waited patiently near his chair.

"Smart dog," Mitch said.

"And an equally clever boy," Katie murmured.

Mitch realized she hadn't missed a thing going on between the boy and dog. She was wearing a bright pink shirt today. It brought out the natural color of her cheeks. Or was it that his presence brought out the rosy hue?

He'd like to believe it was the latter, especially given the way she avoided his eyes.

"How was your morning?" he asked.

She bit her lip and hesitated before giving a pointed glance toward Jacob.

She waited until she sent Jacob to wash his hands in the bathroom before telling Mitch about the slow-moving car.

He stood and walked to the window, scanning the yard and beyond. There was nothing in sight. He eyed Katie's troubled face. "Did you see who was in it?"

"No, it was too far away." She kept her voice low, even though Jacob wasn't nearby. "I only know that the car was a dusty blue."

"Station wagon or sedan?"

She frowned. "Sedan."

After lunch, Mitch called the police station from his office above the barn and reported what Katie had seen.

Unfortunately Mandy didn't have anything to report back.

That afternoon, when Mitch took Jacob for a ride on the tractor, he kept an eye out for any strangers.

He didn't spot any intruders or strange cars, but that didn't mean someone wasn't out there.

Mitch didn't like the idea that someone might be watching the farm.

The notion of being a sitting duck niggled at Mitch long after everyone went to bed.

Relaxing wasn't an option as he heard Katie get up and move around the house.

These days, she slept more than she did when she'd first arrived, but her nightly tour of the house hadn't abated. She always stopped outside his room and lingered in the doorway to watch him sleep.

He would always make himself breathe naturally, so she wouldn't know he was awake. She never ventured inside, but by the time she left, his body was hard and hot.

He often prayed that she'd come to him. But feared if she did, he'd never be able to let her go.

She had no idea what they'd had together. How good they were. How hard it had been to pull out of each other's arms once the day dawned.

Or on some level, did she know?

Was that why she made her nightly pilgrimages? Her mind didn't remember, but her body did?

Maybe he was just fooling himself, trying to make logic where there was none.

If she didn't remember, perhaps this was a sign of her budding feelings for him.

His desire for her cranked up another notch.

At that moment, he heard Katie's bare feet against the kitchen floor. He heard her take a glass from the cupboard and turn on the faucet.

His body was like a tangled knot. Unbearably tight.

He checked his breathing and tried to relax as she left the kitchen and moved toward his room.

The waiting was unbearable. The silence even more so.

He didn't move a muscle.

His head raced with infinite theories and possibilities. Did she want him as much as he wanted her? Why did she hesitate? What was she thinking? Did she ache for his touch?

The clocked ticked in agonizing slowness. He didn't know how long she stood there. When she left, he hurt

in all the places that yearned for what had been denied
too long.

He didn't know how much longer he could stand this
misery.

They spent the entire day at the Wisconsin Dells, and
Katerina didn't know if she'd ever been happier. The
water parks weren't open for the season yet, but they'd
found plenty to do. They'd played mini golf and had
ridden on the amphibious Ducks, boats that traveled in
both land and water. They'd also visited a photography
studio and dressed up in period costumes to have their
picture taken.

Katerina had shot a whole roll of film herself. She'd
gotten used to carrying the camera with her. Her favorite
subjects were Mitch and Jacob, but she also snapped pictures of other tourists, diners in a coffee shop and unusual
land formations common to the Dells.

The day had been lighthearted. She'd never seen Mitch
so relaxed. He let down his guard and was a real person
around Jacob. She knew a good many of her photographs
had been of him. What was hard for her to fathom was
how she could have forgotten anyone so masculine. So
sensitive. So larger than life.

Learning more about the man was becoming an obsession.

She finished off a roll of film just before they left the
Dells.

Jacob was sound asleep by the time Mitch carried him
into the house. Katerina undressed the sleepy boy and
put him to bed.

She ventured into the great room and found Mitch sitting in the big chair. He'd started a fire and the room felt
deliciously cozy. And incredibly sexual.

"I suppose I'd better go to bed," she said, not wanting to leave, but knowing it wasn't wise to stay.

The blue in his gaze snagged hers. "Yes, I suppose you should."

Her feet didn't want to move. She could feel the intangible bond drawing her to him. Her gaze moved to his lips. She remembered all too clearly the taste of his mouth.

"I'm not really tired," she said.

"Yes, you are."

Was that a warning? She wished she could read his thoughts, understand the cryptic message his eyes were sending her. Maybe it was better for both of them if she couldn't decipher his thoughts. It certainly had to be safer.

The room had become unbearably hot.

She started for the door.

"Where are you going?" he asked.

"Outside." She knew she had to get out of the house. "I thought I'd try out the new swing."

"I'll come with you."

He handed her a jacket. She took it, not wanting to tell him that she was too hot to wear it.

Once she stepped onto the porch, the cool night air soothed the heat from her skin.

They crossed the yard together, neither of them breaking the silence. The bright light on the telephone pole illuminated the yard.

Katerina slipped into the swing. She felt the steady strength of Mitch's hands on her backside as he pulled her back and then thrust her gently forward.

The moon shone down on them, making the scene surreal. If she had thought she could keep her heart whole, today had dispelled that fantasy. Mitch's horseplay with

Jacob, his willingness to dress up in silly costumes and his tenderness had chopped a big hole in her weak defenses. He was tough when he had to be. There were times he could be too domineering, but he'd had to be strong and unbendable to make a success out of his cattle breeding operation. Working with this place hadn't allowed for softness or hesitation.

So how had he learned to be such a good role model to a little boy? The caring tenderness seemed as much a part of him as the toughness. There were sides of him that were so like Jacob.

And she was falling head over heals in love with all those precious qualities.

The sounds of the night were the only music to disturb the night. The feelings inside of her were too confusing to be spoken.

They couldn't go on this way forever.

She finally found the courage. "Can I ask you a question?"

"Go ahead." His voice resonated in the night air.

"Tell me about your marriage."

Mitch told himself her interest was a healthy sign. He shouldn't be surprised about her timing. She'd spent the past three days with a little boy. They'd been flirting the edges of being a real family. And at the center of any family was a couple.

He and Katie had been a couple.

"What do you want to know?" he asked.

She used her foot to bring the swing to a stop. Holding on to the rope, she turned the tire around to face him, her eyes wide and questioning. "What was Katie really like?"

The moonlight lit the innocence of her face. "She was

a lot like you. Soft, caring, attentive. She liked kids and was notorious for picking up strays.''

''What are the differences?''

Mitch had to think. ''She wanted to please me, her father, and everyone in the department. I'm not sure she even knew what she wanted. She always wanted to take care of everyone else.''

''That's what attracted you to her, wasn't it?''

Her intuitiveness brought a lump to Mitch's throat. How could he deny what was true? ''Yeah, I think it was. She was genuine. She had a way of wrapping herself around your heart, so you weren't complete until she was with you.''

''Why did you separate? What really drove you apart?''

Mitch had asked himself that question a million times since his wife left. Unfortunately he knew the answer too well. ''I was jealous of your commitment to your job, your father, and everything that got in the way of what I wanted.''

''And what was that?''

''To have you all to myself. I didn't want to share.''

''You were jealous of my father?''

''He was your hero.''

She shook her head. ''He was dead.''

''Becoming a detective brought him to life for you again. I felt like I was competing with your father for your attention.''

Katerina didn't say anything. She stood and faced him, the swing standing between them. She stared into his face, searching for something.

''Are you sure about that? Maybe you were her hero, and she didn't know how to show it.''

"You loved your father more than anything. You told me that on the day we met."

"And what about afterward? After you fell in love? Weren't you her hero then?"

"I don't know. I never asked. I just demanded that you quit what you loved. I wanted you to choose me by forcing the issue of children before you were ready."

"You're very hard on yourself, aren't you?"

"The facts speak for themselves. I lost you, didn't I?"

Katerina's mouth went dry. She was arguing for and against a woman she had trouble relating to. The only thing she could do was try to put herself into Katie's role to see if there wasn't another explanation. "You didn't lose me. It takes two people. Katie had to have made mistakes, too."

"You loved your father, and I tried to take that from you."

"If she put her job before you, then she bore a lot of guilt, too. My father is dead. It's real people that count."

"You don't remember."

"Exactly. I just know what's in my heart."

She clutched his sleeve. Even through his jacket, he could feel the pressure of her fingers. "I can't explain what I did or did not do before," she said. "My memories of my father are precious. But they're like photographs of another time and place. They don't govern what I feel or the choices I'm going to make. No job can ever be more important than having a child or a family. Do me a favor and don't ever compare me to a woman who would do such a thing."

Her fervency was punctuated by her fingers digging into his arm. Talking about having children made Mitch long to pick her up and carry her into the house to make love to her.

"Are you saying you don't want a job outside the home?"

"No, I'm saying I would never put such a job ahead of a child or my husband."

Her adamant stance almost made him a believer.

But this was purely a hypothetical discussion. Katie didn't know what choices she'd make until she could face them.

He doubted that his own mother had intended to be an absentee mother. Yet it had happened.

Katie surprised him by leaning past the swing and brushing her lips against the side of his face. "I think your Katie was very lucky to have you," she said.

He looked at her mouth.

Her tongue nervously moistened her lips.

That was all it took for him to move. He couldn't stop himself. He placed his mouth on hers.

Tentatively at first, she responded by opening her mouth to him. As his tongue mated with hers, he groaned from the pure honey sweetness of her.

She clutched his shoulders as he tasted her.

If they had been anywhere else, he would have forgotten his decision to give her time. The hotness in his blood blotted out the past. He only wanted what was here and now.

Would he be able to let her go if they made love?

No. Not again. That reality ripped through him.

Just as suddenly as the kiss started, he brought it to an end.

Katie's breath came in pants.

For a moment Mitch considered what it would be like to throw his reservations to the wind and haul her back into his arms and finish where he'd left off.

But would such an action be a beginning or a finale?

She broke the silence. "I almost forgot."

"Forgot what?"

"Rafe, the detective who came to see me—"

"I know who Rafe is," he said dryly.

"He called yesterday and asked if I would be interested in helping with a victim's program at the police department."

Her enthusiasm doused his ardor immediately.

"What did you tell him?"

"I wanted to talk to you first."

He gave a rude sound. "Why ask me? Your job always came first."

She stepped back from him. The moonlight caught her stunned fury. "If you can say something like that, then you don't know me. You've still got me confused with another woman."

Mitch realized he'd just blown it. "Katie, I'm sorry—"

She didn't give him a chance to finish. "I am not her. And I never will be."

He could have kicked himself. "I'm sorry. It was a cheap shot."

"Yes, it was." Without looking back, she left.

Mitch heard the door slam as she entered the house. He flinched.

He'd just stuck his foot in his mouth. He wondered if he had just lost his only chance for happiness.

# Chapter 11

He stepped into the house fifteen minutes later and was surprised to find Katie waiting for him in the great room.

"I want to apologize for storming off like that," she said, kneading her hands in her lap.

"It wasn't your fault," he said. "I acted and sounded like a boor. I shouldn't have accused you of putting your job first."

She looked down at her hands. The tight expression on her face didn't ease. She stood, walked around the end of the couch and stopped. "I feel like I'm bumping heads with a woman and a past I can never compete with."

"I don't expect you to be Katie or to compete with her."

"Maybe not, but she's always there. Comparisons are bound to be made."

"What do you want me to do?" he asked guardedly,

not sure where this was headed. Was she going to ask for a divorce again?

"I want you to see me as me."

"I do."

"No, I don't think you do, but I'm hoping you'll want to," she said with a shade of wistfulness and hope.

He swallowed. He'd do anything if it would make her stay. "What are you suggesting?"

"Help me make new memories," she said in a rush. "Pretend we've never met, and we're learning things about each other for the first time."

The relief flowing inside Mitch almost overwhelmed him.

He hadn't dared hope she'd give him another chance.

This time he followed through with his instincts. He joined her in the middle of the room and firmly pulled her into his arms.

"What are you doing?" she asked breathlessly.

He cupped her chin and tilted her face toward him. "I'm giving you my answer."

He lowered his mouth to hers and kissed her thoroughly, erasing everything that went on before and replacing it with the power of the moment.

He had no idea how much time passed. His intent was to make sure that nothing else existed in either of their heads.

He knew he'd succeeded when he lifted his head and observed the confused bemusement on her face.

"That's our first memory," he said.

Her green eyes widened in surprise. She lifted her hand to her tingling lips. Her mouth eased into a trembling smile. "I'll keep it in the forefront on my head," she said. "I'll remember it always."

*  *  *

If Mitch had intended that she think about him and only him, he almost succeeded, Katerina decided the next day.

He'd been the first thing she'd thought of when she'd risen in the morning.

Jacob had to help her keep track of the ingredients for French toast because she kept lapsing off into dream sequences. Luckily, the little boy's memory was completely intact.

Later in the morning, Mitch delivered another packet of recently developed photographs. He didn't stick around long, only to give Jacob a ball to play with and to bestow an intense look on Katerina's lips.

Tears came to her eyes, and he had the audacity to wink before saluting. "I'll see you two at lunch."

"Drat that man," she muttered under her breath.

Jacob gave her a questioning look.

"Sorry, don't pay attention to me. I'm just a little distracted."

He went back to work on the plate of French toast she'd finally made.

She didn't have any appetite, but managed to eat one piece.

Katerina paged through her new photos. She was getting better with the camera. Most of the shots were clearly focused and centered.

Jacob hovered at her elbow, scanning the pictures she'd taken at the Dells. He liked the people pictures best, she decided. He paid particular attention to a photo she'd taken in the coffee shop.

Suddenly his eyes widened and he clutched her hand.

"What is it?" she asked.

He was trembling and staring at the photo as if he'd seen a monster.

She stared at the print. She didn't recognize anyone other than Mitch and Jacob. There were two ladies sitting at a table off to the side. In the opposite corner sat a man with a newspaper partially covering his face.

The boy pointed to the man.

"Do you know him?"

Jacob whimpered.

"Was he involved in the accident?"

He nodded.

"Are you sure?"

He bobbed his head vigorously.

Katerina gave him a hug and put the pictures aside. After she got him involved in a game of tug-of-war with Clancy, she found the detectives' phone number and called the station.

Rafe answered the ring.

She told him about the picture and Jacob's reaction.

"We'll be right out to get the picture. With any luck, someone will recognize this guy from the coffee shop, and we can bring him in."

Mandy and Rafe arrived twenty minutes later. With Katerina serving as the interpreter, they were able to determine that Jacob had seen the man before he'd run them off the road.

Whether he had anything to do with the murder they'd been investigating, they wouldn't know until they interrogated the suspect and discovered who he was and what he'd been doing on the road at that time of night.

As soon as the detectives left, she took Jacob out to find Mitch. If anyone could distract them from a potential murderer, it was Mitch.

She certainly had a hard enough time concentrating when she was with one Mitchell Reeves.

Good news arrived the next morning when Mandy called to say they had a suspect in custody.

"He drives a dusty blue sedan," the female detective said. "It looks like he's the same creep who tried to snatch Jacob from his grandmother's. He has been on parole for armed robbery. We didn't know he was in the area until we got this picture. One of our guys has already picked him up."

Katerina breathed a sigh of relief. "That's great. Maybe that will be the end of our mysterious phone hang-ups, too."

"It should be. This guy usually works alone. Oops, hang on a minute."

Katerina heard Mandy's muffled voice talking to someone in the background.

Then she was back. "The captain wants to talk to you."

Before Katerina could ask why, a deep voice resounded through the phone wires. "Good job, Detective."

"Thank you, but I didn't do that much."

"Yes, you did. You got the kid to open up. We weren't able to get anywhere with him. Victims can be more scared of the police than criminals, unfortunately. I'm hoping you're coming back to work soon."

She shook her head, and then realized he couldn't see her.

"I don't remember any of my training. Any contributions I could make would be minimal at best."

"I wouldn't be too sure about that. We're always hiring outside consultants to get inside the criminal mind.

What's been clear in this case is that we could use some help with relating to victims. You know what it's like to have your whole world upended. People who have been hurt are more responsive to someone who's been in their shoes. Would you be interested in working as a victims consultant?''

Katerina didn't know how to answer. "I don't know. I have to think about it.''

"Mandy and Rafe are already singing your praises with how you've been able to help with the boy. They want you back on the team. We all do.''

"Jacob still hasn't been able to speak.''

"He's been able to communicate to you, and that's what counts.''

As much as the job interested her, she wasn't sure she was the person they needed. What had she really done that could help them? "There are probably other people who are better qualified.''

"Yeah, but you're somebody we trust on this end,'' he said. "The recruits we're seeing these days are listing their personal gang experience on their applications. The worker pool has slim pickings, and it's scaring all of us.''

The flicker of interest kept building inside of Katerina. Working with people would be something she wanted to do. "I still haven't been released by the doctor.''

"Take your time and talk it over with Mitch and your doctor. But we could really use you. You're still on our payroll, and I hate to lose you completely.''

Her mind in a whirl, Katerina replaced the phone.

It rang again.

It was Jacob's grandmother. She was eager to take her grandson to see his new cousin now that the police had the suspect in custody. They would go home in a few days.

While Katerina spent the rest of the morning packing Jacob's things, the boy alternated between excitement and sadness.

Finally, Katerina closed his suitcase and reached over to pull him into her arms. "You can come and visit us anytime you like."

The boy cuddled close to her.

Clancy thrust his furry nose between them.

"I think Clancy wants a hug, too," she said to the somber-faced boy.

He wrapped his arms around the golden-haired dog and hung on for all he was worth.

Mitch entered the room. "Detective Henderson just arrived with your grandmother, Jacob."

The boy leaped to his feet and ran to greet his grandmother.

Katerina took a moment to wipe a tear from her eye before she joined them in the foyer.

"Thank you for taking such good care of him." Mrs. Peterson beamed with emotion. "He looks like he grew an inch."

"It's all those peanut butter sandwiches that he ate," Mitch said, filling in the strained awkwardness.

Katerina was having trouble formulating any words. She was happy for Jacob and his grandmother. Maybe they could start a new life now. But Katerina would certainly miss him.

"You need to thank Mr. and Mrs. Reeves for allowing you to stay." Mrs. Peterson turned her grandson to face them.

Katerina had to bite her lip to keep her smile firmly in place. When he launched himself at her, she sank to her knees and held him tight.

Then she released him so he could go to Mitch.

She saw the sheen of moisture at the back of Mitch's eyes. He blinked it away. His emotions were just as close to the surface as hers.

Rafe bundled the grandmother and Jacob into his car.

As they drove away, Jacob waved from the back seat until they couldn't see him any longer.

Mitch turned to her. "I'm going to miss him." He gazed at the expanse of open space. It seemed more quiet than usual. "I guess this is what it's like for people suddenly faced with an empty nest."

She swallowed the lump in her throat. "If that's what this is, then I don't like it."

Clancy whimpered and sank to the ground. He looked as dejected as Katerina felt.

Mitch grimaced. "We all feel your pain, fella."

Without Jacob's presence, Mitch found himself more on edge than ever. There was no one to defuse the sexual tension spiraling through him.

He tried to keep busy by working on payroll and updating his accounts. But he kept thinking about Katie and what she was doing in the house. How much longer would she be willing to stay now that Jacob had left?

The doctor had hinted that he might release her after her next appointment.

Katie had made giant strides in perfecting tasks. She was still prone to forgetting short-term details. The therapist had encouraged Katie to keep a timer and notepad handy to help her keep focused. With few glitches, Katie hadn't ruined a meal in weeks.

Of course, his appetite wasn't for the food she prepared, it was for having her in his bed.

Mitch turned away from the computer terminal, stood

up and caught sight of Katie with Clancy in the yard below.

Katie had also started driving to and from town. He just hoped her independence didn't represent the beginning of the end for them. He'd noticed a restlessness about her.

The dog was carrying his football, no doubt hoping Katie would play a game of catch. She reached down and took the ball from his mouth. Instead of throwing it, she put in on the ground and gave it a kick.

Mitch grinned. Her kick wasn't much better than her throw. The dog didn't seem to mind. He snatched the ball with his teeth and trotted around the yard before bringing his trophy back to Katie.

She rubbed the back of his head while the dog wagged his tail enthusiastically.

Then she looked up and saw Mitch standing at the window. She said something to the dog and they both started toward the barn.

Mitch felt her presence in the loft before he saw her. Clancy preceded her into the office, toting his prized football.

"Hi," she said, slightly breathless.

"I see you're working on becoming a punter."

"What's a punter?"

"Someone who kicks footballs."

She wrinkled her nose. "I don't think anyone's going to hire me to kick a ball a few feet."

"Don't be too sure. Football teams always need good kickers."

She touched the scar above her ear. "I think I'd rather take the job that the police department offered instead. That sounds more interesting."

Mitch tried to keep his expression bland. "What job is that?"

She told him about the call she'd received from the department. The sparkle in her eye told him her excitement.

When he didn't say anything right away, she tilted her head. "You don't approve?"

"The doctor hasn't released you yet."

"No, but he will soon."

Mitch's gut clenched. "Yes."

And soon could be too soon for him.

Mitch knew cold showers were overrated. He tried them, anyway.

The cold blast did nothing to remove the scent of Katie from his head or skin. He didn't even have to close his eyes to picture her sashaying around the house in her colorful shirts, her bottom fitting snug into her jeans and jumpsuits.

He wondered how much longer he could stand the suspense of not knowing whether she'd stay or go. If she was willing to give their marriage a chance.

He didn't want to make the same mistakes he made before. Just because his mother's job had taken precedence over him didn't mean Katie's would do the same thing.

But the job gave her an option. It still was her ticket to leaving.

Is that what she was looking for? Hell, he'd put up with the job, if she'd just stay. He could understand why she wanted to help a suffering child or a battered woman. She always had the warmth and capacity to soothe others.

When they first were married, it hadn't been an obsession. They both had demanding jobs. They hadn't taken away from the time they spent together. If anything, the times they'd spent together had been more fulfilling. More precious.

Mitch stood under the stream of water and remembered those exhilarating days and perfect nights.

Then something had changed.

She made detective, and everything had gone downhill.

He didn't like remembering the tension between them. He'd wanted the marriage to be perfect. He thought he'd done everything in his power to make sure they were always there for each other.

Katie's enthusiasm for her new position had crept under his skin, he recalled. He had trouble understanding her excitement.

That was when he first suggested they start a family.

She had told him she wasn't ready. She wanted to work a few years first. It wouldn't be fair to either the child or her job to try to juggle the demands of both. When she had a few years under her belt, she'd cut back and devote time to raising a family.

Her rationale seemed unreasonable. He'd resisted her logic.

He took it as a rejection. Why should her job take precedence over their family?

He refused to believe she would ever relinquish any of her job responsibilities.

She'd called him autocratic and pig-headed.

He'd claimed she was turning her back on them.

The painful memories of those heated arguments clawed their way through his conscience.

It didn't take a genius to see what he had done. Katie hadn't been the one to create the tension between them. He had. He'd tried to force her to choose between her job and him because he'd been so scared she'd turn out to be like his mother.

But Katie had never been like his mother. Why had he assumed she would be?

Regret tugged at him.

Mitch slowly turned off the water and reached for a towel.

The cold shower hadn't dampened his desire for Katie. On the other hand, the water hadn't been wasted. He'd faced the truth about the past. Now he just had to find the courage to shelve his fears. Katie had as much right as he did to find a rewarding job.

What she needed from him was his support, not his fear and biases.

He'd tried to control her before and ended up losing her.

He couldn't let that happen again.

Mitch took Katerina out for dinner at the local diner. She appreciated the fact that they wouldn't have to eat in the house without Jacob. Being in the company of other guests eased the atmosphere between them. Mitch kept the conversation light.

After they got home, Mitch disappeared into his bedroom and returned a minute later with a package. He handed it to her.

"What is this?"

"A present to celebrate your one month anniversary at home." His gaze warmed her.

She ripped into the paper and pulled out a photo album with blank slots.

"I thought you might like to use this to store your new memories," he said huskily.

Katerina didn't know when she'd been so touched by

a gift. Did he mean this to be a new beginning for them? Was he starting to forget the old Katie and beginning to see her instead?

She licked her dry lips and grasped the book to her chest. "Thank you. I'll start filling the pages tomorrow."

"That's what I'm counting on," he said cryptically. And then he leaned forward and brushed a kiss across her forehead. "I'll see you in the morning."

Her feet didn't move until after he left the room. Finally she made her way to her own room and sat on her lonely bed. Next to the lamp, she'd placed a photo of Mitch and Jacob riding the tractor. She picked up the print and slid it beneath the clear plastic.

They both looked so happy. Her heart was in that frame. Why was she alone when everything she desired was just a few steps away?

Her heart was still beating rapidly from all the questions spinning through her.

It wasn't the prospect of a new job that captivated her.

It was the prospect of winning Mitch's love, having a family and creating a home together.

Dare she hope they could make a go of it?

She got ready for bed, but sleep was elusive.

She tiptoed across the hall and gazed at Mitch's sleeping form.

An ache in the pit of her stomach budded and grew. She wondered how different it would be if the force of Mitch's love centered on her. He was the type of man who would love unconditionally. He would hold nothing back.

That's the kind of love she wanted.

She didn't want to share it with anyone else. She had to know that he loved her and only her.

He didn't move as she leaned against the doorway. A

few more steps and she could be in his arms. She wanted to feel his arms wrapped around her and the weight of his body pressing her into the sheets. She wanted that more than anything.

She'd seen the desire in his own eyes tonight. In the restaurant, and later when he'd given her the photo album.

They wanted each other. So what was holding her back?

She knew the answer as surely as she knew her name. *Katie. The other Katie.*

If Mitch made love to her, would it be to Katerina or Katie?

Katerina couldn't bear to share him with her past self. She wanted him for her. As she was now.

The longer she debated, the stronger her doubts grew.

There was no choice. She couldn't join Mitch in that bed until she knew for sure that she was his choice, his sole choice.

With a heavy heart, she walked back to her empty room.

# *Chapter 12*

Mitch spotted Katerina in her bright jumpsuit shortly after dawn, as he herded the cows into their stalls.

She'd be hard to miss even if she wasn't a blazing mass of color. He could see her talking to herself as she adjusted her camera lens and snapped a series of pictures. Her presence didn't bother the cows' rhythmic cud-chewing. He, on the other hand, had a hard time keeping his mind on the tasks at hand.

Throughout the day, she followed him wherever he went. She shot footage of him pitching hay, changing the oil in the Jeep, and gazing at the pasture.

Later that evening when he came in to eat dinner, he found her adding another role of film to her camera.

"I'm beginning to feel like centerfold material," he said, with a quizzical grin. "Maybe I should take you to town so you can find a new subject."

"The only subject I'm interested in is you," she said.

"I'm making memories so I'll never forget you," she said seriously.

The bit of bread Mitch had just eaten lodged in his throat. "It sounds like you're getting ready to leave. Are you?" He had to ask, even though he didn't want to hear the answer.

She shook her head. "I'm not leaving, unless you want me to."

"I don't."

She gave him a wide smile. "Then I won't."

He noticed she didn't promise forever, but he'd be grateful for today. "So why are the photographs so important?"

"The moment when I took these is already past, but I have a photograph to keep it alive forever. It gives me a piece of history and allows me the luxury of remembering again and again."

She looked so happy at the thought. He thought she'd never looked sexier.

Mitch didn't dare breathe. Was his imagination starting to play tricks on him, or was that desire he saw simmering in the green depths?

He blinked and looked at his plate. He'd been too long without sex. That was the problem.

She put down the camera and pulled a chair across from him.

He looked up. Her gaze was leveled on him.

"Is something wrong?" he asked.

"No. I'm just wondering what it's like to make love to you."

He'd thought he could handle anything: the short-term memory losses, her color preferences, her midnight forays through the house. He'd managed to keep his desires in check whenever she'd reach for him or shadow him from place to place.

His defenses weren't as thick as he'd thought. Nothing had prepared him for her simple desire.

He tried to clear his throat. "What are you curious about?"

She leaned forward. The neckline of her jumpsuit shifted and he could see the gentle curve of her cleavage. "I want to know what it's like to be your wife."

"Why?"

"How can I know what I've forgotten if I can't try to recapture it?"

He shook his head. "This isn't a good idea."

He picked up his plate and hauled it to the sink. Without looking at her again, he started putting dishes into slots in the dishwasher. He ran the water to rinse his glass, hoping the sound would drown out the roar in his ears. It didn't.

He shut off the faucet and turned. Katie stood right at his elbow.

"Why isn't it a good idea?"

His response was glued in his throat, behind a wall of fear.

He couldn't treat making love casually.

If they made love, he wouldn't want to stop. There had to be more than sex. More than a quick release. He wanted it all: the future, the two point five kids and the pair of matching rockers. If she decided to walk away afterward, he'd be destroyed. He needed to cling to the hope that she'd fall in love with him again. Then he wouldn't have to worry about holding any of himself back. He could love her with the heart and intensity he was capable of.

"Why isn't it a good idea?" she stubbornly repeated.

"The doctor hasn't released you yet." The excuse sounded lame.

"But—"

"I'm going to take a shower," he cut her off, desperately attempting to forestall the argument forming on her stubborn lips.

"You just took one," she protested.

"I need another one."

He didn't wait for her rebuttal and left her standing in the kitchen as he stormed into the bedroom and headed straight to the shower. He flung off his clothes as he strode through the room.

He twisted the nozzle to release the water and stepped into the lukewarm spray.

Before he could turn the nozzle to a colder setting, the door of the shower opened.

"The doctor never said I couldn't have sex," Katie said.

The woman was too stubborn for her own good.

"He probably forgot to mention it." Mitch tried to shut the door.

She wouldn't let him. Neither did she attempt to hide her curiosity of his body.

She slipped by him into the shower, the water drenching her orange jumpsuit and plastering it to her body.

Mitch almost groaned out loud. "Katie, could we talk about this another time?"

"Are you thinking about her?"

"Her?" For the life of him he didn't know who she was talking about.

"The other Katie."

"Does it look like I'm thinking of anyone else but you right now?" His body was in agony.

Her eyes widened at the sight of his growing manhood. "Oh, my. Does that hurt?"

"Like hell."

"What can we do to make it better?"

He gritted his teeth. "Katie."

"If it's not her that's stopping us from making love, then you must not want me." She sounded miserable.

Damn. It didn't matter that Katie didn't have a clue about men and why they reacted the way they did. He yanked her into his arms and kissed her with all the heat and purpose he'd been deliberately stifling. The luke-warm stall steamed.

If he feared she'd run screaming from him, he couldn't have been more wrong.

She matched his kiss with innocence and fervency. When he slipped his tongue into her mouth, she enthusiastically allowed him entrance and matched him stroke for stroke.

Mitch tried to maintain control. She wouldn't let him. Her hands found him and cupped him.

He pulled back from her, his breath ragged and harsh. "Do you have any idea what you're doing?"

"Katie had a part of you I've never had. I'll never know unless you make love to me. I need this for me. For us, if there's ever going to be an us."

"This isn't another photograph for your collection?"

She moved against him, her body already learning the rhythm to enticement. "I don't want just pictures any-more," she said softly. "I want the real thing. I learned all about you, but it's still not enough. I need you to show me who you are, and what we can be together."

He couldn't fight both her plea and the raging urgency of his own body. He turned off the water. Pushing open the door, he grabbed a towel and wiped her down. Then he pulled off her sodden clothes.

She attempted to dry him off. But he was too impatient.

He swung her into his arms and carried her into the bedroom. They landed on the bed together, his body following hers onto the mattress.

She reached up and grasped his head, pulling it to hers. Whatever she didn't remember, she made up for intuitively and by inventive exploration.

Mitch didn't know when he'd ever been so turned on. Her hands were untutored, but she willingly followed his lead.

He cupped her breast, and she arched toward him.

"Katie," he rasped the minute she found his nipple and tasted it with her tongue.

Mitch had relived their lovemaking many times in his dreams. But dreams didn't match reality. He had forgotten how exquisite her touch was. How soft she was. What energy she brought to simple foreplay.

He felt as if he was trying to contain a wildfire and was losing the battle.

Katerina sought to relieve the teasing ache between her legs. She didn't think she'd ever seen anything more beautiful than Mitch's naked body. In her mind, he shouldn't wear clothes. He had too many fascinating parts that she wanted to see in the light of day.

She loved the whiskered feel of his mouth against her. He was hard to her soft, and she reveled in the sensations twisting between them.

When his hand touched her breast, bright lights flashed through her head. This must be heaven. Wild, with all the colors of the rainbow. Why had they waited?

"Tell me where to touch you," she breathed against

his mouth. Her hand drifted lower, but he wouldn't let her touch him.

"Show me how to please you."

"You're doing fine."

She wiggled, impatient to ease the niggling itch inside of her.

He grabbed her hands and clasped them over her head, forcing her to give up control.

"Mitch, please," she begged.

He ignored her begging and gave himself to the pleasure of relearning her secrets.

Katerina didn't know there were so many sensuous nerve endings in her body. He found each and every pulse point and made it throb with his mouth, his tongue or the scrape of his whisker.

The heavy weight of his manhood rested against her leg. She longed to touch it, but his grip on her hands made it impossible. Instead, she could just whirl through the universe he was unveiling.

His head lowered to her stomach. He kissed the hollow of her belly and went farther.

She finally managed to free her hands and clasp his hair. "Isn't it my turn?"

He stopped and gazed up at her, his breathing ragged. He squeezed his eyes shut and gave a quick nod.

She didn't wait for him to change his mind. She splayed her fingers across the muscled smoothness of his chest. The raw firmness of his body intrigued her. She tasted him and kissed as many parts of him as she could reach. Her tongue couldn't discern any differences among food groups, but it took detailed notes of the unique flavors of this man. She felt like a sponge, absorbing every detail, every nuance of the way their bodies fit together, and every sound Mitch made when she caressed his hot skin.

She'd just begun her journey of exploration past his navel when he stopped her and turned her onto her back.

"I was just getting started," she protested.

"And so am I." His gaze contained a wicked glint.

He slid his fingers into her, making her arch toward him. The ache cascaded into a stringent need.

The wetness between her legs grew.

Just when she thought she'd go out of her mind with desire, Mitch lifted himself over her and plunged into her.

Her legs wrapped around him as he sank deeper inside. She stretched and basked in the sensation of being filled. Grabbing his shoulders, she matched his movements. He felt enormous and perfect.

The blue of his eyes plumbed her soul.

Everything inside her kept building. She wanted more.

His rhythmic pace was maddening.

The intensity on Mitch's face mirrored the fierce beating inside her.

Suddenly the core of her body reached the top and exploded into a thousand stars. Mitch tensed and gave a muffled shout into her ear.

They fused together, both absorbing the delicious aftershocks. Each breath he took echoed the pulse of her heartbeat.

Katerina didn't know how long they stayed locked together. She was worn out and exhilarated at the same time. Her hands continued to caress the wide breadth of his shoulders. She couldn't get enough of him.

He had filled an enormous void inside of her. She no longer felt empty. She felt warmed and nurtured. Was this what their relationship had been?

Why hadn't they made love sooner?

Mitch knew how good they were together. He had to have wanted this more than she did.

"You are the most incredible woman I know, Katie my love," he murmured into her ear. "I love you. You make my life complete."

Happiness surged through her. She snuggled deeper into his arms, reciting his words in her head.

"You always call me Katie."

"That's how I think of you. You'll always be Katie."

When had "always" started?

And how did Katerina fit into the "always" picture?

Did he love her as he had Katie? More? Less?

Katerina tried to banish the words and the doubts. She should be happy with the way things were. Making love to Mitch had been so incredibly right. She didn't want anything to ruin it.

But the voice of fear took form and became strident.

*Katie. He wanted Katie.* She was still between them, in this room.

Mitch lifted himself from her and rolled onto his side, pulling her close to him.

For a moment she closed her eyes and let herself drift, postponing the questions starting to rear inside her head. She wanted to just bask in this supernatural world for a little longer. If only they could banish the past and everything that had happened up to this moment. That would make it all so perfect.

Mitch couldn't have moved if his life depended on it.

He had been afraid that if he'd unleashed the full storm of his desire, Katie would be overwhelmed. That hadn't happened. If anything, he was the one overwhelmed. She had been real and enthusiastic. She hadn't hid what she needed or wanted. Her honesty had always been a cornerstone to her personality.

But mixed with the innocence of her zealous enthusiasm, they were a toxic potion.

She stirred in his arms.

"What are you thinking about?" she asked.

"You." He propped his arm under his head and gazed down at her.

"Do you think…" Her voice trailed off, and she turned away.

Was she embarrassed?

He used the tip of his finger to ease her face toward him again. His self-satisfied pleasure faded as he saw the questions hovering in her green eyes.

"Katie, what is it?" He didn't like the doubts he was feeling. "Are you regretting that we made love?"

She shook her head. "No. It was wonderful. Better than I imagined it could be. And I have a terrific imagination."

"Then what's wrong?"

She bothered the scar over her ear, something she seldom did anymore. "Do you think you could ever love me as much as you do the other Katie?" She rushed on before he could answer. "I know it's asking a lot because you have a whole history with her. But I'd like to know if I'll ever have a chance to be first…" Her voice trailed away.

Mitch couldn't believe what she'd just said. He didn't want to believe it. Trying not to rush into judgment, he carefully formulated his response. "There is no other Katie. There's only one you."

She moved away from him, so there was a cool space between them. "Did you think about her when you were making love to me? Or were you thinking about me? Only me?"

He tried to keep his frustration from taking charge of his temper. "I was thinking of you."

"So you didn't compare what we did now to what you had with her?" Her green eyes didn't cut him any quarter. They demanded honesty from him.

Mitch didn't like where this conversation was going. The width between them seemed to be growing, even though the sheets were still warm and damp from their passion.

"Katie—" he began.

"I'm Katerina," she interrupted. "Why can't you see that?"

Suddenly she pulled away and sat up, but not before Mitch saw the tears sliding down her cheeks.

He tried to reach for her, but she eluded him.

She grabbed for his shirt that was lying on the floor and yanked it on.

"Katie—er, Katerina, I don't see that there's a difference. Yes, there are changes between the way you were before the accident and how you are now, but they're superficial." He flinched and wished he'd found a better word.

She buttoned the shirt and looked at him with a pained expression. "Did you love her?"

No matter what he said, it was a trap. He had no choice but to give her the truth. "More than anything in the world."

She clenched her fists. "And what about me?"

"Nothing has changed. I still love you more than anything in the world." Desperate, he sat up. "I love *you*. No one else. It's always been you."

Her shoulders sagged. The animation died from her face. "Then that's that."

"What are you saying?"

"I don't know if I can live with you, not knowing if it's the other Katie or me that you really love." She angrily brushed aside another tear. "I know this doesn't make sense to you. I know we're one and the same. But I want you to love me as I am now, as I will be tomorrow. If it's the other Katie you want, eventually you'll be disappointed."

"That's not going to happen."

She walked into the bathroom and returned with her clothes.

"Where are you going?" he asked.

"To my room. I've got to be alone to think."

She left before he could stop her.

Mitch dropped back to the sheets and stared up at the ceiling.

In the background he heard the ominous ticking of the clock. He wondered how something so wonderful could have gone so wrong.

Had he betrayed his love to Katie? Everything he'd ever accomplished paled in comparison to his wife and his love for her.

He loved Katie. He loved Katerina. They were different, and yet so much alike. Both of them were part of the whole in his mind. She couldn't remember how it was between them.

His memories were precious. It bothered him a lot that a blow on the head had been all it had taken to erase what they had together. It was unfathomable that some part of their lives hadn't survived, even though she could remember parts of her youth.

But the past few weeks had provided a new configuration of just who Katie was. She thought of herself as Katerina, but he could see so much of Katie in her. Fundamentally she hadn't changed as a person. Deep down, she was still Katie. Warm, nurturing and tenacious. Even when she was in the convalescent home, he'd been drawn to the extraordinary strengths she'd used to get back on her feet. The staff had commented on it, as well. She'd learned fast and worked hard to perfect her skills.

Her kindness and encouragement of others had also earned her recognition. Those hadn't been a surprise to Mitch, either. Why should they be?

He could wonder if Katie had always had a penchant for wild and crazy colors. Or if she'd always been this inquisitive.

It wouldn't surprise him if these hidden facets of her personality had been there all along. The way she was today blended into what he knew about her in the past.

He didn't want to let go of what they had. It was a part of him, of them.

Why couldn't Katie see that?

Was she using this as an excuse to leave?

He'd thought it would be her job that would come between them. But that wasn't the case; this time she was using herself.

He couldn't quit loving Katie, no matter what she called herself.

How could he convince her the past was no threat unless she was looking for an excuse to remove herself from him?

Maybe that's what he truly feared.

Katerina paced inside her room as Clancy kept track of her back-and-forth treks.

She knew she shouldn't begrudge Mitch's memories of his wife and his marriage. She tried to tell herself that she didn't. He had a right to the special recollections.

But where did that leave her?

How could she ever believe his confession of love? She wanted to believe him. Being loved by Mitch would make everything else worthwhile. Assisting the police detectives would be a perk, something to share with him at the end of the day. She'd have something extra to bring to their relationship.

Loving Mitch would be the foundation. She could survive any hit by fate if she had him by her side.

But if she couldn't count on his love, then she would be trusting a fantasy. What looked like an oasis would be hallucinatory.

She wanted to believe he loved her. Yet, how did she know his love was centered on the fact that he had loved Katie first? He had a desire to still love her. So he couldn't see that they were different. Was he overlooking their differences because he didn't want to see? Would he still overlook them ten years from now? Or would doubts and regrets set in?

If he did see her unique qualities, could he ever appreciate them?

Fantasy and reality. Which one characterized Mitch's feelings?

Katerina still felt the incredible bliss from their love-making. The experience had shaken her to the root of her being. It was everything she'd longed for and more. What she couldn't have guessed was how much hungrier she'd become. She couldn't be content with less than the whole package. She wanted Mitch. His love. His home. His family. She wanted to share a life with him that would include the highs and lows, the good and the bad.

She stopped her pacing and stared at the dog, who was silently watching her. "How will I know if I can trust what he says?"

Clancy just looked at her.

He didn't have any answers, either.

She didn't know what to do. She knew she'd hurt Mitch with her doubts, just as she was hurting. He didn't deserve this any more than she did.

In another week or so, she had to make a decision about what she was going to do.

They couldn't go on this way.

She was afraid that whatever she decided could hurt both of them.

# Chapter 13

Katerina would have found the next week frustratingly lonely if it hadn't been for Rafe and Mandy. The two detectives arranged to pick her up and bring her to the department to get acquainted with how they handled victims.

There were awkward moments during the first few days. She didn't remember most of the detectives' names. They were surprisingly tolerant of her mistakes. She got lost in the building a few times. Fortunately someone always managed to track her down. Using the drills she'd learned during her therapy, she conquered her glitches. Bit by bit she was getting a handle on the job. Despite her fear of failing, she was starting to enjoy working at the department.

During the middle of the week, she rode with Mandy to visit a robbery victim. The middle-aged woman was terrified and kept getting her facts confused.

Katerina didn't know what was expected of her or how

to help the investigators. While the officers checked the premises, Katerina just talked to Mrs. Helms, the older woman who was still distraught over the invasion of her home. Katerina followed her instincts, encouraging the woman to share insights about her life. Katerina asked about her family and discovered the woman's husband had died the year before. The woman started to relax her grip on the chair as Katerina shared the challenges her own mother faced following the death of her father.

The woman perked up and quit twisting the handkerchief she'd been holding. She talked about her marriage and how they'd only had each other since they had no children.

She stared down at her hand and started to cry. "I hadn't taken off my wedding ring since the day my husband put it on my finger."

"Where is it now?"

"He took it and put it on his own finger. His hands were dirty and greasy-looking, as if he worked on cars." She rubbed her small finger as if she was trying to get rid of something.

Mandy came up behind Katerina. "He put it on his little finger, Mrs. Helms?"

The woman nodded.

"What did the ring look like?"

"It was a plain gold band about a half inch in diameter."

"Was there an inscription?"

"It said, 'Mine.'"

A short time later after they left Mrs. Helms, Mandy congratulated Katerina.

Katerina didn't think she deserved any credit. "I just talked to her. I don't see how that helped you."

"She hadn't told us about where he put the ring or

what his hands looked like. You were able to get some pertinent pieces of information because she trusted you. That was more than she could give us when we walked into the house.''

Katerina produced a sad smile. "I felt sorry for her. She's lost so much.''

"Yes, but she gained a friend today, didn't she?'' Mandy gave her a shrewd glance.

Katerina didn't deny it. She thought she'd call Jacob's grandmother to see if she would be willing to stop by. Mrs. Helms needed companionship right now. The two women were about the same age.

Katerina was exhausted by the end of the day. She managed to be asleep by the time Mitch came into the house each evening following chores.

They were at an impasse. She wished she knew how to hurdle the wall between them.

She still couldn't sleep through the entire night. At one o'clock in the morning, she found herself wandering the halls. But now she steered clear of the master bedroom. She didn't trust herself to go near Mitch's bed. Her memories of her brief sojourn in that room were crystal clear in her mind. She didn't trust her willpower. It would be too easy to slip into Mitch's bed and arms.

And in truth nothing had changed. She still didn't know if Mitch could ever love her.

Jacob's grandmother brought him to the farm on Saturday while she went to her monthly card club.

The weather was unnaturally warm for a spring day. With thunderstorms in the weather forecast and an increasingly gloomy sky, Katerina decided they shouldn't venture too far from the farmhouse. They played a couple of games with Clancy. Mitch stopped in briefly to put together a puzzle with Jacob. After that he excused himself and went out into the barn.

Jacob fell asleep on the couch in the middle of the afternoon.

Suddenly a big clap of thunder shook the house.

Jacob woke with a startled cry.

Katerina had been in the kitchen, cleaning the counter when she heard him.

She raced into the room and pulled him into her arms. His little body shook with fright.

"It's okay, sweetie. Just a lot of bluster and noise, nothing more."

"I couldn't…" He started to speak and then stopped.

Katerina couldn't believe what she'd heard.

"What couldn't you do?" she asked quietly, keeping a firm, soothing hold on his quaking body.

"I couldn't wake her up." His voice sounded raspy and raw.

She had to strain to hear the faint words. "Who couldn't you wake?"

"Mommy."

Katerina's heart started to race. "You tried to wake your mommy?"

He gave a strangled sob. "The car pushed us off the road, and I tried to wake her, but my voice wasn't loud enough. I wasn't big enough."

Katerina saw the blame and anguish in his tear-drenched face. She shook her head. "Jacob, your mother didn't die because of you."

The little boy's expression didn't change. If anything he appeared more dejected. "No. It was my fault."

Katerina looked confused. "Why do you think that?"

"Because when the second man came—"

"Second man? There was more than one man?" She

spoke slowly so he wouldn't misunderstand the importance of her question.

He nodded soberly. "The second man wore dress-up clothes and carried a mean-looking gun."

Katerina was afraid if she stopped talking, so would he. He'd been holding all his emotions inside. There was probably a proper procedure for addressing this situation. Unfortunately, she didn't know what that would be.

"Did the second man come with the first man?" she asked.

The little boy wrinkled his nose as if he was thinking real hard. "No. He came later."

"He didn't see you?"

"I hid under Mommy's coat."

"Then what happened?"

He frowned. "He walked around the car before he reached in and touched my mommy."

Katerina assumed the touch meant the man was checking for a pulse.

"Do you think if I had yelled at him, my mommy might still be alive?" The boy's lip quivered and two fat tears leaked from the corners of his eyes.

Katerina gathered him close and rocked him in her arms. "No, honey. Your mommy was already gone. There wasn't anything you could do to help her."

She didn't know if he heard her or not. He was sobbing openly now.

Mitch, who had come through the door in time to hear Jacob's confession, moved toward them.

Before he could say anything, she mouthed at him to call the department. She didn't want to leave Jacob. He needed to vent his grief.

Jacob's hurt ran deep.

As Mitch left the room to contact the police, Katerina

cradled Jacob until he fell asleep in her arms. When she heard his breathing even out, she let her own eyes drift shut. His emotional breakdown was every bit as taxing to her.

Mitch returned to the great room following his call to Rafe. After Mitch gave Jacob's account of the accident and the second man, Rafe reported the detectives had already suspected there was a second person involved. However, they had no concrete evidence.

Jacob's eyewitness account was a much-needed break.

Up until now, the police had only been able to file a hit-and-run charge against the suspect they had in custody. They hadn't been able to link him directly to the murder scene that had been less than a mile away from the accident. This new information gave them a solid lead.

Rafe promised to keep Mitch posted as soon as he knew anything. He also would make arrangements to increase the patrols by Jacob's grandmother's house again. They weren't going to take any chances with Jacob's well-being. The guy with the gun probably thought he was in the clear. Jacob's safety could be at stake if the killer learned otherwise.

Mitch took the time to speak to Jacob's grandmother. She was concerned, but determined not to panic.

Standing in the doorway of the great room, Mitch found Katie and Jacob snuggled together, sound asleep. Katie had her arm tucked protectively around the small child's shoulders. Even in her sleep, her natural caring and warmth were evident.

Mitch quietly crossed the floor. He leaned over, snagged the blanket from the end of the sofa, and covered the sleeping pair.

Then he sat in the big chair and watched them both.

Lately, knowing Katie could undermine his famous control with the blink of an eye, he'd been trying to keep his distance—for both their sakes.

But now he'd have to deal with circumstances over which neither of them could determine the outcome. His inability to whisk Katie and Jacob out of harm's way made him feel powerless.

All he could do was stay close and hope the police got their man sooner than later.

Staying close to Katie would play havoc with his libido. He was having a hard enough time keeping his hands off her.

He had no idea how long he could keep all his desires in check.

Katerina reluctantly relinquished Jacob to his grandmother.

Since he'd awakened, he hadn't quit talking, and his grandmother seemed more excited about his speaking again than concerned about the extra police protection.

Jacob didn't seem bothered about having a police escort, either; he considered all the detectives his friends.

As they drove out of the farmyard, Katerina returned Jacob's exuberant waves. When the car was finally out of sight, she caught sight of Mitch and immediately felt the tension that she had successfully ignored return. There was no way she could disregard the intimacy they'd shared.

As Mitch headed toward the barn, she entered the house. Wherever she went, her awareness of Mitch followed. His work boots in the entry, his shaving cream in the bathroom. All the pictures she'd taken of him were scattered throughout the house and the images crowded her head. It was time, she decided, to bring some order to her chaos.

She sat down at the table and picked up a stack of photographs. She memorized every angle of his face as she slipped print after print of Mitch into the photo album he'd given her. There was a depth and passion in his expression that had started to haunt her dreams at night.

The want to be with him as a woman was growing, making her desperately needy.

She set aside the photo album and drifted to the window. Staring down the bluff, she traced the meandering river's path, steady and sure. That river followed the same course, from one season to the next. There was little deviation.

Katerina never thought she'd yearn for the mundane. She hankered for color, excitement, and moving forward. Today she'd give anything for peace and surety. She wanted to escape the probing questions and the paralyzing doubts.

Why couldn't she just go with the flow and take what was there?

Why couldn't she forget the yesteryear of Mitch with Katie?

The answer came to her in a blinding flash.

She was jealous. She would never know what it was they'd had. She could never share in the enriching memories or understand the foundation those memories had provided for the future.

She was jealous of Katie because that woman had had Mitch's heart first and foremost. Katerina wondered if she'd ever appreciated what she had.

Probably not. Katie had left Mitch.

Katerina couldn't imagine what would drive her to do that.

At the same time, Katerina didn't know how she could stay and live in Katie's shadow. She didn't want to be second in Mitch's affections.

She wanted to be first.

How could that ever happen? She didn't know how she could ask Mitch to choose between them. That wouldn't be fair to him.

And the other woman wasn't here to defend herself.

It was late when Mitch finally came into the house, a week later, weariness forcing him to abandon his book-keeping.

He headed for the great room and discovered Katie curled up on the sofa, sound asleep.

Mitch's fists curled at his sides as he took in her exhausted features. Katie had been working steadily for a week. There were dark purple circles under her eyes. She looked thinner in the bright red T-shirt and matching pants.

Guilt charged through him.

Damn, he'd been so busy trying to keep his distance, he hadn't paid attention to the toll the stress was taking on her.

When Katie came home from her days at the police department, she was usually exhausted. The work wasn't particularly difficult, but he knew she still had to work hard to keep her thoughts focused on the task at hand. Her short-term memory losses would be a permanent life-long condition that she refused to let deter her from working.

On top of the day-to-day cases, he was certain Katie worried about Jacob, and the fact that the police hadn't been able to identify the second gunman who had shown up at the accident scene. The detectives were trying to keep a lid on their evidence and Jacob's eyewitness account, but the first suspect's attorney was applying pressure to get the charges dropped.

He was certain Katie's worry had increased when Jacob's grandmother had reported that the hang-up phone calls had resumed. The police were trying to trace them but hadn't had any luck.

Mitch stared hungrily at Katie's pinched features. How much longer could they go on like this? She'd been here almost two months.

Something had to give. But he was scared to force the issue.

Making love had driven Katie further from him.

Now she was avoiding him by working. He tried to convince himself it was better for both of them if she kept busy. So why did he feel abandoned?

Mitch sighed. He couldn't leave Katie on the couch, he bent and gathered her sleeping form into his arms to carry her to bed.

She barely stirred as he entered her bedroom and laid her gently on the bed.

Katie opened her eyes. She didn't seem surprised to see him. She offered him a smile that made his stomach flip-flop and caused him to break out in an urgent sweat.

"You are the sexiest man, I know," she whispered huskily.

"Don't say that," he growled. Heaven help him—he didn't have the energy to walk away from her when her green eyes looked like sun-kissed leaves.

"It's true. All the men in the department are good men, but they don't have your lips, your brilliant blue eyes and your incredible body."

"Katie." He groaned.

"I think about you all day, even when I'm trying not

to,'' she said wistfully. She lifted her hand to his face and stroked his lips. "I think about how good we were together in bed. Do you think about it, too?"

He couldn't answer. His body was in a flame of need.

She must have seen the hot truth in his eyes. "What are we going to do?"

He searched her warm, open face. He knew what he wanted. What he needed. Reaching for her hand, he brought it to his lips. He kissed the inside of her palm. Then he lifted his head. "Stay with me, Katie. Let's put the past behind us and start over."

Tears started to fill Katie's eyes. "I want to, Mitch. More than anything, I'd loved to say yes."

"Then say it," he demanded, trying to blot out the fear that was gnawing at him. He could feel her fear and doubt.

She didn't answer. Instead she searched his face. She pulled her hand to trace the contours of his jaw.

He couldn't breathe.

Finally her hand fell away. Anguish drenched her eyes. "I need time. I know I'm not being fair, but I need to be sure."

"Sure of what?"

"Sure that I'm the one you really love. I know the other Katie will always be there, but I've got to find a way to deal with that. And right now, I'm not having any luck."

The words were a shot to his soul. How could he separate the past from the future? She resented what she couldn't remember. And he didn't want to give up those times.

Despite his instincts to hold her close and never let her go, Mitch pushed away from the bed.

He forced his feet to walk out the door. How he found the willpower to leave, he didn't know.

For the rest of the night, he counted the minutes ticking on the clock. He heard Katie leave her room in the wee hours of the morning to wander the house. But this time she didn't come near his room.

His bed was lonelier than it had ever been.

# Chapter 14

The next morning Katerina noticed that Mitch seemed to be hovering over her. He wasn't usually indoors from sunup until noon.

She'd overslept and walked into the kitchen to find Mitch stirring up a batch of waffles. Under his watchful eye, she attempted to eat at least half of the portion he'd heaped on her plate.

"Do you want some eggs with that?" he asked.

"No, this is fine." She pushed her plate away from her.

"You should eat more." He sat across the table from her and gently slid the plate toward her.

"I've had plenty."

"It doesn't look that way." He gave her body a critical eye.

She felt instantly self-conscious. "What's wrong?"

"You look thin."

"I've lost weight. It'll come back soon enough." She

reached up to massage the back of her neck, which had been sore since she'd gotten up.

Her answer made Mitch's mouth flatten into a stubborn line.

Whatever he would have said got lost in the shrill ring of the telephone.

Mitch answered it, then handed the receiver to Katerina.

"Good morning, Katie," Rafe said, his voice strangely professional, void of his usual joviality. "We've got a lead in the homicide. Milwaukee picked up a guy who was driving the murder victim's car."

"Did he run Jacob's mother off the road?" she asked, as Mitch came up behind her and began kneading the tight muscles in the back of her neck.

"He's denying it," Rafe said, his tone indicating he'd heard that excuse before. "Says he bought the car from a friend. It doesn't matter what his pitch is, we need to have our little kid check out a police lineup to see if he can finger this guy for us."

"You're taking Jacob to Milwaukee?"

Mitch's fingers worked like magic, even though she was having trouble concentrating. It was hard to keep her mind on anything else when Mitch had his hands on her.

"We're leaving in an hour." Rafe's voice jarred her awake again. "The captain has requested you come with us to Milwaukee. Jacob's grandmother can't go, and Jacob trusts you."

She straightened. "An hour?"

"Can you make it?"

"Just a minute."

She pulled away from Mitch's fingers and gave him a quick summary of Rafe's request.

Mitch looked at her. "Do you want to go?" he asked.

"Yes. I can't let Jacob go by himself."

"I'll drive you."

Katerina didn't know why Mitch agreed to accompany them to Milwaukee, but she was relieved he would be there.

As difficult as their relationship had become, she knew she could rely on him for support.

It wasn't the only thing she wanted from him. The long hours during the night made her all too aware of the other things she'd like from him. For now, however, his support was the only thing she'd allow herself to take.

Jacob didn't act nervous about going to a strange police station. He chattered nonstop from Bakerstown to the outskirts of Milwaukee. Once they got inside the big city, his brown eyes widened and he twisted his head every which way to see all the sights.

"Can we go to the zoo?" Jacob asked, as they drove by a big billboard adorned with monkeys, giraffes and penguins.

"Not today." Katerina kept her voice light. She was more nervous about what lay ahead than he was. She prayed this would be the end of the little boy's nightmare. She loved seeing his enthusiasm for life return.

"Can we go another day?"

"Perhaps. We'll have to ask your grandmother."

"She'll say yes," he said with supreme male confidence. "She likes monkeys."

Mitch met Katerina's gaze over Jacob's head. The boy's unabashed enthusiasm brought smiles to both their faces. The moment of sharing warmed Katerina.

Mitch's head swung back to the road. He was following Rafe's unmarked car; they'd decided to bring two separate vehicles so Rafe could stay to question the suspect. They'd all agreed that they didn't want Jacob hanging around the police station any longer than absolutely necessary.

Jacob lost some of his animation when they entered the station. Several officers took them through the halls and had them wait in a private room. The D.A. and another man, whose name Katerina couldn't remember, had already come in to talk to Jacob about what to expect.

Jacob fidgeted in the big chair next to Katerina's, his feet dangling over the edge.

"Will I have to talk to the bad man?" he asked her when everyone else had left the room.

She took his small hand into hers. "He won't even see you. You'll be behind a window that he can't see through."

"Is it a magic window?"

"Something like that."

Jacob worried his lip with his teeth and kept a strong grip on her hand.

"Will you stay with me?" he asked, sounding young and achingly vulnerable.

Katerina struggled to keep control of her emotions. She prayed her leaky tear ducts would obey her command just this once. "I'll stay with you the entire time."

Only one tear eked out of the corner of her eye, but she managed to brush it aside without much ceremony.

Jacob scuffed his shoe against the chair leg. He twisted toward Mitch. "Will you be there, too?"

Mitch shook his head. "They didn't invite me, but I'll wait for you right here. Afterward, we'll stop for ice cream. How does that sound?"

Jacob grinned. "I like chocolate ice cream best."

"Then we'll have to find chocolate." Mitch reached

over and mussed the boy's hair, making him squeal with laughter.

Rafe came into the room. "Okay, fella. It's time to go."

Katerina thought they looked like a funeral party as they filed solemnly into the dark, somber room.

Jacob clutched her hand tightly.

Standing in front of the window, he seemed so small to be handling such a big responsibility. In his white shirt and dark pants, he looked like a little adult. It wasn't hard to imagine this child staying with his dead mother through a long, dark night of pain.

Katie hoped he could reclaim his childhood as soon as this ordeal was over. She longed to see a mischievous twinkle in his dark eyes.

Jacob stared into the window. "Take your time," one of the attorneys in the room said.

Katie didn't look at the men in front of them. Her attention focused entirely on the little boy she wanted to protect. If he showed any signs of being upset, she vowed to whisk him from the dark room, no matter who it annoyed. He was just a child. A child who had been through too much.

Except for a serious frown, Jacob didn't show any sign of distress. He firmed his sturdy chin and stared hard at each suspect on the other side of the glass. A district attorney and several lawyers had crowded into the room with them, but no one interrupted the boy's intense concentration. Everyone seemed to be holding their breaths.

Finally, Jacob turned toward Katie and shook his head. "I don't see him. He's not there."

"Are you sure?" Rafe asked.

The boy nodded. "Yes. None of those men came near my mommy."

Katie kept her own disappointment in check. "Come on, then. Mitch promised us ice cream."

"I want chocolate." Jacob gave her a toothy smile, but retained a tight grip on her hand. That was fine with Katerina; she didn't intend to let him go.

He didn't loosen his fingers until they found Mitch and left the building.

Once on the sidewalk, they waited for the light to change before entering the crosswalk of the street in front of them. Jacob jumped up and down excitedly between them, clutching both their hands. His shirttail had worked its way loose, and he was beginning to look more like a six-year-old boy than a little man.

"You okay?" Mitch asked her.

"I'm fine," she said as calmly as she could. There was a giant lump in the back of her throat, making it hard for her to talk normally. Her eyes burned from fatigue and intense disappointment. She hadn't realized how much she was hoping this interview would be the end of the ordeal for her little friend.

She had so hoped this interview today would bring closure to his misery so he could start rebuilding his life. He deserved to have a happy childhood just like any other child.

She kept her fears and desires buried, not wanting Jacob to be burdened with her frustration.

She wanted him to go home to his grandmother happy and carefree, even though a killer still could be out there, watching and waiting.

The light changed, and they stepped from the curb and proceeded across the street. The big buildings loomed on either side of them. Horns honked. Jacob skipped between them and sang a little song.

They were halfway across the intersection when Katerina heard the sound of squealing tires and a racing engine.

She looked up to see a big black pickup bearing down on them.

She reached instinctively for Jacob.

Mitch grabbed them both. He shoved them forward and threw himself on top of them as the vehicle passed, just missing them in their crouched position.

A powerful suction pulled at them as the pickup raced past.

Katerina gasped for air, her ears hurting from the pounding of her heart.

"Come on, let's get off the street," Mitch yelled.

He half carried them as Katerina, her legs wobbling, clutched Jacob to her, refusing to let him go.

As soon as they reached the curb, a crowd of concerned passersby pressed close, asking if they were all right. She nodded. Jacob just shivered in her arms.

Then she heard a loud train horn wail in warning.

Brakes squealed.

Boom!

Katerina couldn't see what was happening with all the people surrounding them. It sounded like metal slamming into a solid wall.

She hugged Jacob to her. A siren screamed.

The crowd grew larger around them.

She looked up and realized she could no longer see Mitch.

Panic hit her.

"Mitch?" she called.

She didn't see him in the sea of strange faces. Her heart beat wildly in her chest. "Mitch!"

"Katie, I'm okay. I'm right here."

She heard his voice before she saw him wedge his body through the tight circle of people.

He sank to his haunches and pulled them both into his arms. "Are you okay?" he breathed into her hair.

She couldn't answer. She could only rock Jacob in her arms and give thanks they were all safe.

Her heart hammered as Jacob wiggled in her arms.

She loosened her hold slightly and looked into his white face.

"What happened?" he asked. "Why did that truck try to hit us?"

"I don't know, but the main thing is we're all okay." Mitch lifted Jacob into his arms while helping Katerina to her feet.

A young-looking police officer arrived on the scene.

"You folks okay?" he asked.

"We're fine." Katerina gave him a weak smile.

The officer gave her a sympathetic nod. "Glad to hear it. We'll need a statement from you before you leave."

Mitch looked ready to argue, but Jacob piped up first, "Do you have any chocolate ice cream?"

The young officer stroked his chin. "I think we can find some. Do you want it in a bowl or cone?"

"A cone."

Katerina couldn't help herself. She hugged Jacob again.

"You're the bravest little boy I know," she whispered into his ear.

"And you're the bravest lady I know," he whispered back loudly.

Katerina grinned at his little face. His skin appeared pale, but he was twisting in her arms and craning his neck to see the commotion down the street. He was already recovering from their near brush with death.

If only adults could mend their hearts and lives so quickly, she thought.

A quick glance at Mitch's stoic expression brought the truth home to her that what a child wished for and what an adult knew were two different things.

They didn't leave the police department until several hours later, much to Mitch's disgust. He hated waiting in small rooms. He also didn't like all the paperwork and endless questions. He understood what needed to be done. But he wanted nothing more than to get Katie and Jacob out of this city for once and all.

They were both relieved Jacob wouldn't have to face any more lineups.

During their wait, they'd learned the grim answers to the events that had transpired.

The driver of the black pickup was dead. After failing to run them down, he'd raced around a railroad barricade and hit a freight train. He died upon impact.

His identity hadn't been released, but Rafe told them confidentially that the dead man had been a well-known district attorney in the running for state supreme court.

The Milwaukee detectives were already grilling the suspect they had in custody. And even though he was angling for a plea agreement, the police had been able to piece together the events of the Bakerstown murder and the resulting accident that had killed Jacob's mother.

The DA, whose name was Grant Mears, had hired a local con man to kill a suspected drug dealer. Mears had ambitious plans to run for public office, but he needed to cover his past drug habit. He didn't want the press snooping around and discovering his secret, so he arranged to have his former drug supplier killed.

After fleeing the crime scene, the killer spun out of

control and ran Jacob and his mother off the road. He called Mears to report the shooting was a done deal and to tell him about the accident. The killer insisted the woman was dead because he'd stopped and checked. But Mears wasn't the trusting sort. He hadn't wanted to risk leaving any loose ends. He'd driven out to the accident scene to make sure there were no clues or witnesses to his association with the murder. It wasn't until he'd read the Bakerstown police reports that he learned of a possible witness. The D.A. used his contacts in the department to learn Jacob's identity and to keep abreast of the investigation.

Rafe believed a thorough investigation and the bartered testimony of the hired killer would reveal the connection between the drug dealer and the D.A.

Jacob, who had been quietly playing with toy cars in the corner of the room, came over and climbed into Katerina's lap. A big chocolate ring jaggedly circled his mouth. There were also several drips of chocolate dotting his once-white shirt.

"I saw the bad man," Jacob said solemnly.

"Yes, you did," Katie said gently. "You were very brave to stay with your mommy and keep her safe."

"No, not that day," he insisted. "I saw him two times."

Mitch hunkered down to Jacob's eye level. "What other time did you see him, Jacob?"

The little boy's brown eyes glistened as he met Katerina's eyes. "I saw him at the police station on the day you fell down the steps."

"You saw me fall?" Katerina asked.

He nodded. "I was hiding at the bottom of the stairs next to the garbage can. I wanted to tell you about my mommy, but then a man who was wearing handcuffs got mad and started yelling. He came charging down the steps. You tried to stop him, but he knocked you down. You fell.'' Jacob's lip quivered. ''I tried to warn you, but the words got stuck here.'' He pointed to his throat.

Katerina cupped her hand tenderly under his jaw. ''That wasn't your fault, Jacob. There was no way you could have stopped my fall even if you could have warned me. It all happened too fast.''

''It was a good thing you'd stayed hidden,'' Rafe inserted. ''If you'd yelled, you might have put yourself into greater danger.''

The little boy sniffed and glanced from one adult to the next, as if he wasn't sure whether to believe them or not.

Mitch ruffled his hair. ''You showed a lot of courage. If I have a son someday, I want him to be just like you.''

Jacob peeked up at him, hesitant. ''You do?''

Katerina thought she'd never seen anything more beautiful than the sight of Jacob's tentative smile. She didn't try to stop the errant tear streaking down her face. ''Your mother would be just as proud.''

''She would?''

''Absolutely.''

The boy threw his arms around her neck.

''How did you manage to sneak into the department? Why didn't anyone ever see you?''

Jacob's gaze shifted away guiltily. Then he shrugged. ''The first day I came, I hid behind the big trash can. There was so much noise, no one saw me.''

''And the other times?''

He clamped his mouth shut.

''Someone let you in, didn't he?''

Jacob's eyes got big. Katerina knew she had hit the nail on the head.

"Was it Detective Rafe?"

The boy squirmed and nodded. "He wasn't doing anything wrong. He said I was probably easier to keep track of at the station than I was outside, so he let me in. I also made friends with the doorman. They won't get in trouble, will they?"

"I'm sure Captain Loomis already knows." Now she knew why no one was making a big deal out of the boy's sudden appearances. They'd chosen to let the boy in so they could keep an eye on him. She doubted this conformed with any department regulations, but who was going to report them? And to whom? They'd all done their part to keep the little boy safe.

Katerina felt a warm glow spread through her.

When they arrived at his grandmother's house, Jacob gave big kisses to both Mitch and Katerina before he raced into his grandmother's arms.

For once Katerina didn't have anything to say as they drove the short distance home. Mitch was lost in his thoughts, as well.

Inside the house, Katerina stopped Mitch from heading to his room to change clothes by laying her hand on his arm.

His dark, intense face seemed remote. But she knew differently. She'd seen the many sides of the man. She still wished she knew them all, but that would take a lifetime of being together. And she didn't know if she was ready for that.

"Thank you for saving our lives today," she said quietly. "We all would have been killed if you hadn't acted so quickly and strongly."

His eyes revealed little, traveling down to where her

hand was now linked with his. The paleness of her skin stood in stark contrast to the tanned tones of his.

He placed his palm over her fingers. "You don't have to thank me. You're my life, Katie. Without you, it has no meaning. I'd rather be in the path of that freight train than to ever lose you again."

Katerina didn't know what to say. Words trembled on her lips. Words that were frozen in place by fears. But did she dare say them?

Mitch gave her a gentle push toward her room. "You look exhausted. Why don't you go to bed? Butch helped with chores today, and I've got to relieve him so he can go hang out with his buddies. We'll talk later."

Katerina watched him leave, mesmerized by the hard planes of his face, the slips of gray in his hair and the firmness of his walk.

Somehow, at some time, he'd become the center of her world.

She didn't want him out of her sight. Today she'd seen how quickly life could change.

She only had to think back on the day, recalling that one brief moment when she'd heard the collision and lost sight of Mitch. She'd been paralyzed by her fear that something had happened to him. He was a man, after all. Just flesh and blood like any one else. As vulnerable to injury or worse, as she had been.

She understood about loss in that flicker of an instant. She understood the suffering Mitch must have endured when he'd thought she might not live.

Since her accident she'd only known what it had been like to be the person waking up with no memories, trapped in a fervent search to discover who she was.

She'd become single-mindedly focused on her quest to

make sense of her confusing world, impeding her awareness of anyone else's pain.

She'd granted few concessions to the depth of Mitch's feelings. She had been so sure his love for Katie was blind. But she was beginning to understand the dimensions of such a love. The heart had no boundaries. If she'd lost Mitch today… She wouldn't have cared if he'd been crippled or had suffered a head injury—her feelings for him wouldn't have changed.

She had been blatantly unfair to Mitch.

He'd never wavered in his commitment to her. And he had refused to deny the past, even though he loved her.

Katerina had been so busy trying to define his feelings, she'd refused to see the full scope of his love.

She wasn't sure how she could make it up to him.

# Chapter 15

Dr. Norton set down the chart. "I'm sorry to say this, but I think I'm going to have to dismiss you, Mrs. Reeves. Except for routine checkups, or any health problems, you shouldn't have to come back for six months."

Mitch listened to the doctor's beaming pronouncement and felt his blood go cold.

His time had run out.

Katie could go to back to work full-time, and she'd be free to live on her own.

What would she do?

Katie had kept her gaze trained away from him, and he couldn't tell what her decision would be. Her subdued response didn't obliterate her warm extension of gratitude to the doctor and his staff.

Five minutes later they left the doctor's office and climbed into Mitch's car.

"I'll catch a ride home with Rafe," Katie said after Mitch pulled into the police department's parking lot.

"We're going to work on the final report of Jacob's accident."

"Are you coming home after that?"

She shook her head. "I'm going with Mandy to talk to an elderly victim who has been abused."

Before Mitch could question her any further, Katie opened the car door and slid out. She hesitated briefly, as if she might say something, but changed her mind.

The door closed.

She never turned back to look at him as she hurried into the building.

Mitch's fingers coiled tight around the steering wheel. His chest hurt.

Katie was fleeing as if the devil were on her tail. She was making it clear she'd rather be here than with him.

Why shouldn't she? He'd been so scared this would happen; he'd all but pushed her away.

Just as he'd done before. Why hadn't he learned? Why had he let fear instead of common sense control him?

Mitch's chest hurt from the emotions he'd suppressed. He should have congratulated her on her accomplishments and told her how proud he was.

Instead he hadn't said more than two words to her since they'd gotten up this morning.

He could have lost Katie if that car had been any quicker or he'd been any slower.

Was he going to live with regrets for the rest of his life?

Had he lost her for good this time?

It would serve him right if he did.

A raw hunger built inside him. He needed his wife back in his bed for good. He didn't care if her name was Katie or Katerina. He just wanted his wife back.

* * *

Mitch moved around the heifer. Her tail was lifted, and there was still no sign of the calf. He had a feeling this wasn't going to be an easy delivery.

Butch had already left to attend a wedding.

The other farmhands also had commitments. Hiring high school students had its benefits unless there was a school dance. Tonight was the prom.

Katie slipped into the barn about seven o'clock, with Clancy sticking close to her side.

"Aren't you going to come and eat dinner?" she asked.

"I can't leave this cow. She's not presenting herself right."

Katie came into the stall and gingerly touched the protruding belly. "What does that mean?"

"It means she's probably breech."

Katie stayed back. "Why don't I bring your dinner down here?"

"You don't have to do that."

She put her hands on her hips and glared at him. "I want to help."

He straightened. He hadn't seen her flash of temper in a long while.

In the past he would have shut her out and they'd both end up mad. That hadn't gotten them anywhere.

Mitch analyzed her stance and the determined glint in her eye. "I would appreciate some dinner."

She seemed surprised at his acquiescence, but she relaxed. "I'll be right back."

"Katie?"

"Yes?"

"If you want to help, you should put on some different clothes."

She gazed down at her potent pink pants and shirt. "What's wrong with these?"

"Not a thing. But they weren't made for calving. A pair of jeans will hold up better."

She nodded and smiled.

His gut tightened as she left.

By the time Katie returned, Mitch didn't have any interest in food. The heifer was becoming more agitated, moving uneasily from side to side.

"What's wrong?" Katerina put down the tray and came into the stall.

He had rolled up the sleeves of his denim shirt and was pressing his hands to the cow's side. Whatever he felt didn't please him. "The calf hasn't turned."

She tried to gauge the seriousness of the situation by analyzing the expressions on Mitch's face. He appeared to be gritting his teeth. "Do you want me to telephone the vet?"

"I already did. He was out on another call."

The cow gave a distressed sound as water gushed from her.

Mitch moved around the cow. "Grab the rope off that post."

Katerina pivoted and spotted the coil of rope.

As soon as she handed it to Mitch, he said, "Find the ladder and bring it here."

She managed to find the wooden ladder at the other end of the barn.

Dragging it into the stall, Mitch positioned the ladder below a broad beam.

"What are you doing?" She couldn't keep her questions inside any longer.

"We need leverage to help pull the calf out." He offered her the end of the rope. "Climb up and hook this rope over the beam."

Katerina didn't stop to ask any more questions. She could see the heifer becoming more and more anxious. The tension in Mitch's face told its own story.

As soon as Katerina found the end of the rope and hooked it over the beam, she dangled the end in front of Mitch. He grabbed it and pulled it toward the cow.

By the time she got off the ladder, she saw Mitch quickly wrapping the rope around the suddenly visible hooves of the calf.

The cow's agitation grew.

Katerina didn't know if there were any sounds other than their labored breathing and the cow's restlessness.

As soon as Mitch attached the rope to the legs of the calf, he started to pull. Katerina saw the strain of his arm muscles as he used his weight to pull the calf from his mother's body.

Katerina couldn't stand watching. She slipped around Mitch and used her own weight to help.

For a long moment it seemed as if their efforts were for naught. Nothing moved.

Then slowly the calf began to emerge.

"That's it, sweetheart," Mitch growled. "Keep coming, keep coming. You're doing great."

Whether he was talking to her or the cow, Katerina didn't know. She matched her movements with his.

Then it was over. The calf emerged.

Mitch laid the calf next to its mother.

Katerina couldn't move as she watched the calf resting, stunned by her own sudden arrival.

Then the calf rolled its eyes.

Her first breath came in a jerk.

Katerina released her own, realizing how tense she'd been.

The calf started to squirm and its mother flipped her massive head around and began to lick her new infant.

The more the calf moved, the more interested the mother became in her newborn.

Katerina couldn't take her eyes from the scene in front of them.

"How long before the calf will stand up?" she asked.

"Twenty to thirty minutes at least. Since she was breech, she'll be weaker. It might take her longer."

Time ceased to exist. Katerina sat on the bale, continuing to watch the miracle unfold.

Both seemed healthy and content. It was hard to believe that only an hour ago they were locked into a life-or-death struggle.

The animals didn't suffer the angst and what-ifs of nature's twists. With nary a blink of an eye, they assumed life as if it were a matter of destiny, having made the adjustment and now moving on.

Katerina had no idea what time it was when the calf, after a half dozen attempts, managed to climb to her feet.

"She's beautiful," Katerina breathed. She didn't think she'd seen anything more delightful than the wobbly legged, homely creature.

Mitch leaned against the pitchfork he'd been using to spread straw across the thick mat and lime lining the stall.

"Yeah, she is," he agreed, his tone thick with emotion.

Katerina looked up and saw that his gaze wasn't directed toward the cow or her new calf. His eyes were focused entirely on Katerina. Blue crystals beamed a powerful wave of emotion.

She couldn't stop a tear from sliding down her face.

Mitch reached over and caught it with the tender pad of his index finger.

She no longer saw the animals. Mitch filled her vision. Dominated her senses.

She couldn't look away from him if her life depended on it.

Her fingernails dug into her palms. "You saved the calf's life."

"With your help."

She nodded. "We're good together, aren't we?"

He nodded. "Yes, we are."

The calf bleated a mournful ma-a-a, reminding them of its presence.

"Why don't you go in and get cleaned up," Mitch suggested. "I'll finish up here."

Katerina looked down and saw that her clothes bore the visible signs of their labor. Mitch looked just as grimy.

She grimaced. "I need to take a shower."

"Don't use all the hot water," he said.

She blushed at his suggestive look. For once she was tongue-tied.

Mitch heard Katerina's departure. He finished spreading the straw and watched the calf sink to its bony knees to curl up next to his mother. The cow chewed contentedly, as if it was all in a day's work to her.

Mitch had witnessed countless births. Each one was special. But this one would live in his mind forever. He'd shared it with Katie.

He knew it wasn't his imagination that a bond had formed between them.

Katie had never spent much time on his cattle operation before her accident. She hadn't had time. Or perhaps, he'd just never invited her.

He was used to carrying the load alone. He wondered if that hadn't been the crux of his problem. He was used to being boss, but not sharing his thoughts.

He had effectively pushed Katie aside. He'd made demands, but hadn't been willing to give in return.

Something cracked open inside of him and allowed him to take a hard look into his soul.

Over the past few days he'd had a chance to observe Katie at work. She was good at what she did. Damn good. Her relationship with Jacob and her ability to relate to people in need were a special part of her personality. She'd blossomed and grown. He had to admit, he'd been impressed.

He'd been a jerk to insist she give up her job. What had ever possessed him to be so blind?

She didn't use her job to put distance between them. She never had.

He'd been so blinded by his own insecurities and determination to control their future that he'd all but pushed her into leaving him.

Mitch moved toward the door.

It had taken Katie's accident to bring him to his senses. Her job hadn't been a threat to their having a family. He had tried to force something because of what his mother had chosen. That hadn't been fair to Katie. She had gifts and talents that could never be utilized on the farm. Why had he insisted life be just on his terms?

Mitch could see now that her job had never been the issue.

His fears were what had gotten in the way. He'd tried to overcome them by forcing her back to the wall.

He'd learned the hard way that he couldn't control life

any more than he could stop a cow from having a breech delivery. There were no guarantees.

Katie wasn't his mother. Katie had too much love and emotion inside of her to make the same mistakes his mother had made. Her protectiveness toward Jacob had revealed the depth of her maternalism. A child would always come first with Katie.

Mitch knew he had a decision to make.

The key to his future was in Katie's hands. It wasn't any simpler than that. Or any more uncertain.

Would she give him another chance?

Standing beneath the stream of water, Katerina could feel all her muscles tightening from her intense exertion. Yet she felt more alive than she could ever remember.

She'd witnessed a new life being brought into the world. What a beautiful affirmation of life.

Mitch had given her credit for assisting him, but she knew that he had done all the work. His fierce determination to bring that calf safely into the world stayed with her.

When the calf had emerged from her mother's womb, Katerina had felt as if she'd been the one to give birth. A bond had been created between her and Mitch.

The past ceased to exist.

Only she and Mitch had been in that barn. They had built an important memory between them, one that joined with their adventure in Milwaukee and their mutual caring of young Jacob.

She had worried for weeks about being compared to Katie. What a waste. Mitch hadn't tried to make her into someone else. Katerina had been the one thrusting the past between them.

Katerina turned off the water and grabbed her towel.

Wiping her hair vigorously, she found herself smiling.

She wasn't afraid of her own shadow anymore, because the future didn't have any shadows. The past was truly over. Whatever she needed to know, she'd ask Mitch or her mother or whomever.

All that she wanted was to be with the man she'd grown to love. The only memories that mattered were the ones she could make with him.

She blew her hair dry, then pulled one of Mitch's old shirts from a hanger and slipped it on. She couldn't resist looking at herself in the mirror. The woman that beamed back at her was confident of who she was.

Whether she was Katie or Katerina didn't matter.

Katerina turned off the light and left the room. She could feel her pulse pounding as she crossed the floor to the master bedroom.

Easing through the doorway, she saw Mitch emerge from the bathroom. He wore a towel around his waist and was still damp from his shower.

He stopped when he saw her. His gaze widened appreciatively at the sight of her attire and her bare feet.

He opened his arms, and Katerina met him halfway.

Pulling her tight against his damp chest, he buried his face into her hair.

"I missed you," he said.

She lifted her head. "What did you miss?" she asked. She wanted to know everything about him: how he thought, what he treasured, and what he needed.

"I missed not hearing how your day was when you worked with that robbery victim. I missed not having you by my side in the morning and not hearing you sing in the shower. I missed watching you choose what outlandish, colorful outfit you were going to wear. And I missed having you sleep in our bed."

Katerina's eyes started to well. Each one of his memories was about Katerina, not the old Katie.

Katerina waged an inner battle to hang on to her composure and found herself losing the skirmish. In desperation, she put her hands over his lips to halt his words. "Stop," she begged, half laughing. "You're making me cry, and I'm tired of turning into a watering can, over every little thing."

The blue in his gaze gleamed with male devilishness. He pressed a kiss to her fingers and pulled her hand away from his mouth. "I like the idea that you get all soggy over me. You've got the most incredible dewy green eyes."

"You do it on purpose?"

"How else am I going to have my way with you?"

"Is that what you want?"

He shook his head. "I want whatever makes you happy."

"And if I continue to work with the police department?" she asked. "I can't give that up. It's important to me."

He nuzzled her ear. "I'll keep your side of the bed warm until you get home."

"Do you still miss the old Katie?" She couldn't keep herself from asking.

"I have wonderful memories of those years, but that's all they are—just memories. You were always strong, confident and compassionate. That has never changed. Yet, we've both changed and grown."

He kissed the sensitive skin below her ear before raising his head again. "Life doesn't stand still. We both made mistakes. What matters is who each of us is now, and the choices we make. I choose to be with you and to love you forever. Katie, I love you, and I always will."

Katerina heard the conviction of his love. She knew she'd never doubt him again.

"I love you," she said, delighting with the naturalness of the words as they rolled from her tongue. Desire built and hummed at the core of her body. "And what about when we have children?"

"You want children?" he asked.

"I want to have lots of children. We need to fill up this big, empty house."

"I'm in no hurry." He pulled her closer to his body and lifted the back of her shirt with his hand to caress the sensitive hollow in her lower back. "Let's wait a year or two."

"Are you sure?"

He nodded. "Very sure. I'm not ready to share you yet. I've suffered through too many nights of listening to you parade through the house instead of being tucked in next to me. I don't want to share you with a baby's demanding schedule."

"You heard me wandering through the house?" She couldn't contain a blush.

"I was in agony." He chuckled and blew gently in her ear. "But each time you stood in that doorway, it gave me hope that someday you'd choose to stay instead of just lingering there."

"I want to stay now." She lifted her face to his.

He brushed a kiss across her lips before stepping back.

"What's wrong?" she asked.

"We need to do something first. I want to make this official."

He turned to the nightstand and pulled open the drawer. He reached for something and faced her again.

"Put out your hand," he said.

She did what he asked.

He slipped a ring onto her finger and raised it to his lips. "I had your old wedding ring reset. It has something old and something new."

He gently pushed her so she sat on the mattress, facing him.

Then he went down on one knee and asked, "Will you be my wife, Katerina, my love?"

The tears filled her eyes. "I'll be your wife, if you'll be my husband."

"Gladly." Mitch rose to his feet and lifted Katerina into his arms. His lips met hers as they sank into the bed.

Katerina had no idea what the other Katie did to capture such a wonderful man. But Katerina would be grateful for the rest of her life that she was smart enough to marry Mitch.

# *Epilogue*

Mitch tugged at the tight button blocking his windpipe. The shirt was every bit as uncomfortable as the first time he'd worn it.

He had no complaints. Today was their fourth wedding anniversary, and the second time he was going to pledge his vows to Katie.

"Are you ready?" the minister leaned over to ask him.

"More than ready," Mitch said. He'd been ready for Katie all his life.

The minister gave the signal, and the music started.

Mitch turned to face the back of the chapel.

Jacob led the way past the small group of family and friends, his face solemn and intense. The almost seven-year-old boy, his hair combed neatly and parted just-so, wore a new suit and carried a small heart-shaped pillow with the wedding rings. He tried to keep time to the music, but wasn't overly successful.

Mitch winked at him as Jacob marched in front of him and then came to stand beside him.

"How did I do?" the boy whispered.

Mitch winked at him. "You were great."

Jacob beamed, revealing a toothless gap in the front of his mouth. He looked like a typical, happy kid dressed in the penguin suit. The worried circles had completely disappeared from beneath his brown eyes. During the past year, he'd put on a little weight and had grown at least two inches.

He still liked visiting the farm and playing with Clancy, but his visits were growing fewer and farther between.

Though Katie tried to see Jacob whenever she could, she'd had to concede he was growing older and had more activities in his own age group.

Mitch knew Katie would always have a special place in her heart for Jacob, but she'd soon be busy with their own little one.

The music changed, and Mitch's pulse picked up its own beat.

In the doorway of the church, Katie glided toward him. She looked like an angel, except the angel wore a bright blue dress with matching headpiece. She'd hunted for weeks for the perfect dress. She'd finally found what she was looking for in a catalog.

The dress was typically Katie.

As Katie floated down the aisle, no one could question her feelings. Her smile filled her whole face. She greeted people on either side and gave a hug to Jacob's grandmother. As she turned, Mitch saw the telling swell against the dress. They'd planned to wait for their family, but nature and their frequent lovemaking had decreed otherwise. Neither of them minded. They both wanted a child to share the love they had for each other.

Mitch noticed Katie kept a protective hand over her belly as she greeted Rafe and Mandy. They also earned big hugs.

Mitch loved watching Katie be Katie. She no longer referred to herself as Katerina, claiming that "Katie" sounded more intimate and personal. Mitch couldn't agree more.

Toward the front of the church, Katie's mother and her new husband were the last to receive Katie's warm brand of welcome. The mother of the bride was just as teary-eyed as her daughter.

A photographer snapped another picture. Katie had instructed him to take photos of each and every one of the guests who were scattered throughout the sanctuary. Mitch eagerly anticipated the nights when they could cuddle in front of the fireplace and relive these moments.

Katie finally arrived at his side.

"Am I late?" she asked with a twinkle of her green eyes.

"Never. You were just on time," he said, meaning every word.

On cue, her eyes moistened. She reached for the hankie she had tucked into her sleeve. "You do that deliberately, don't you?"

"Can I help it if I love to bring you to tears?"

She flung her arms around him and pressed her lips to his. Mitch wrapped his arms around her.

In the background, the minister cleared his throat and a uniform chorus of chuckles resounded throughout the congregation.

Mitch refused to be hurried. He had all he wanted in his arms.

He'd learned to take advantage of each moment, and take advantage he did, kissing his wife as if there were no tomorrows.

Jacob sat next to his grandmother at the center table and watched Mitch and Katie dance while contemplating the probability of asking his grandmother for another piece of cake.

Jacob thought this wedding stuff was cool—not as cool as soccer, but still kinda fun.

Mitch had given Katie a bicycle built for two for a wedding present. Jacob thought that was an awesome present. He couldn't wait to get married.

Katie had ordered chocolate wedding cake because that's the kind Jacob liked best. He'd asked for the piece with the most frosting. Katie had made sure it was also the biggest.

His grandmother said Katie and Mitch spoiled him, but his grandmother smiled when she said that.

Jacob still missed his mother. But he and his grandmother talked about her a lot. And at night, he talked to his mother when there was no one else about. That's when he felt closest to her. She listened just the way she always had.

Jacob saw Mitch swing Katie around the dance floor. She had that glimmery look on her face again. She did that a lot around Mitch.

Mitch made Katie happy. That made him more than okay in Jacob's eyes.

They were going to have a baby, and Jacob was going to be his honorary brother.

Jacob's chest swelled with pride whenever he thought about it. He'd make a good brother.

He'd also make sure no bad guys ever came near his

brother or sister. He'd protect him just like Katie and Mitch had taken care of him. He might even be a detective like Katie was. Or maybe he'd work with Mitch. He liked the cows and stuff, too.

Jacob shrugged. He'd talk to his mother about it sometime after he ate another piece of chocolate cake.

\* \* \* \* \*

# SILHOUETTE

# SENSATION®

## AVAILABLE FROM 15TH JUNE 2001

### MISSION: IRRESISTIBLE  Sharon Sala

*A Year of Loving Dangerously*

Agent Alicia Corbin's mission was to persuade brooding SPEAR operative East
Kirby to return to the field as her partner. Their aim was to catch a traitor, *not* t
get emotionally involved!

### THE RETURN OF LUKE McGUIRE  Justine Davis

Luke McGuire had been everything shy Amelia Blair was fascinated by but too
wary to go too near. But now he was a reformed character—even if he still
looked dark and dangerous!

### DADDY BY DEFAULT  Nikki Benjamin

Gabriel Serrano lived quietly, raising his son Brian—until a mysterious woman
appeared on his doorstep, staking a claim on his house. What did this tempting
beauty know about what had happened ten years ago?

### A STRANGER IS WATCHING  Linda Randall Wisdom

Three years ago Jenna Welles had entered the Witness Protection Programme
and left the man she loved, but now the criminals had found her and once mor
she had to trust Riley Cooper with her life—but not her heart!

### BLADE'S LADY  Fiona Brand

For years hunted heiress Anna Tarrant had dreamed of a secret hero. Now,
about to emerge from hiding to claim her fortune—if she could evade her wou
be killer—Anna encountered Blade Lombard in the flesh…

### GABRIEL IS NO ANGEL  Wendy Haley

Locating a fugitive should have been simple for Rae Ann Boudreau, but that v
when she ran into a sexy brick wall named Detective Gabriel MacLaren… It
seemed *he* was hot on *her* trail!

**AVAILABLE FROM 15TH JUNE 2001**

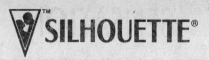

# SILHOUETTE®

## Intrigue

*Danger, deception and suspense*

**A MAN OF HONOUR** Tina Leonard
**LITTLE BOY LOST** Adrianne Lee
**A MOTHER'S SECRETS** Joanna Wayne
**ONE GOOD MAN** Julie Miller

## Special Edition

*Vivid, satisfying romances
full of family, life and love*

**THE PINT-SIZED SECRET** Sherryl Woods
**IN SEARCH OF DREAMS** Ginna Gray
**THE SHEIKH'S SECRET BRIDE** Susan Mallery
**MILLIONAIRE TAKES A BRIDE** Pamela Toth
**WILD MUSTANG** Jane Toombs
**THE BRIDE SAID, 'FINALLY!'** Cathy Gillen Thacker

## Desire

*Intense, sensual love stories*

**THE RETURN OF ADAMS CADE** BJ James
**SLOW WALTZ ACROSS TEXAS** Peggy Moreland
**RANCHER'S PROPOSITION** Anne Marie Winston
**SHEIKH'S TEMPTATION** Alexandra Sellers
**THE DETERMINED GROOM** Kate Little
**THE BABY GIFT** Susan Crosby

0601/18b

# Silhouette Stars

## Born this month

Tony Curtis, Bjorn Borg, Tom Jones, Judy Garland, Boy George, Dorothy L Sayers, Steffi Graf, James Brown, Catherine Cookson, Kathleen Turner.

## Star of the month

# Gemini

The underlying emphasis this year will be self discovery and throughout this period you should make progress in all areas of your life. You may have to say goodbye to a close friend, but be assured that other relationships will more than compensate the loss.

SILH/HR/0601a

 **Cancer**

You are still feeling optimistic and in love with life, ready to enjoy all that is happening around you. Finances may need to be handled with care to avoid curtailing your plans.

## Leo

There is plenty on offer and the trouble will be finding enough time to do everything you want. Relationships may be strained mid-month; however, a small gesture on your part will ensure a happy outcome.

 **Virgo**

A social, relaxed month which restores your energy levels ready to take on the world again. A special occasion late in the month brings an old flame back into your life.

## Libra

This month starts brilliantly with relationships back on track and a special evening brings passion into your life. Career matters need careful thought, as you may not be offered what you deserve.

**Scorpio**

A pleasurable month with relationships going from strength to strength and you could be ready to make a stronger commitment. A trip abroad will be very productive if linked to work.

## Sagittarius

Definitely the month in which to keep your options open, as there could be some exciting opportunities coming your way. A friend lets you down, but they may not understand your reaction.

 **Capricorn**

Recent financial gains put you in the mood to change your surroundings, but consider all the options as a quick decision may not be the right one. A special person lets you know how much they care.

## *Aquarius*

Your self esteem rises during the month and you will find people are attracted by your confidence. Romantically an excellent time to get more intimate.

 **Pisces**

Time to take a break and reflect where you want to go as you have been wasting time and energy on misplaced plans. A loved one offers support, so listen, as they may have the perfect solution.

## *Aries*

After the hectic whirl of the previous month you will need to take time out to restore your energy levels. A friend has news that makes you wonder about someone close.

 **Taurus**

Problems at work may overspill into your personal life, so confide in those close rather than leave them wondering. Late in the month an opportunity to change direction lifts your spirits.

*Look out for more*
*Silhouette Stars next month*

# FREE

## 2 BOOKS
### AND A SURPRISE GIFT!

We would like to take this opportunity to thank you for reading this Silhouette® book by offering you the chance to take TWO more specially selected titles from the Sensation™ series absolutely FREE! We're also making this offer to introduce you to the benefits of the Reader Service™ —

★ FREE home delivery     ★ FREE gifts and competitions
★ FREE monthly Newsletter     ★ Exclusive Reader Service discounts
★ Books available before they're in the shops

Accepting these FREE books and gift places you under no obligation to buy; you may cancel at any time, even after receiving your free shipment. Simply complete your details below and return the entire page to the address below. **You don't even need a stamp!**

**YES!** Please send me 2 free Sensation books and a surprise gift. I understand that unless you hear from me, I will receive 4 superb new titles every month for just £2.80 each, postage and packing free. I am under no obligation to purchase any books and may cancel my subscription at any time. The free books and gift will be mine to keep in any case.

SIZEC

Ms/Mrs/Miss/Mr ..........................................................Initials..............................

BLOCK CAPITALS PLEA.

Surname.............................................................................................................

Address.............................................................................................................

.........................................................................................................................

.............................................................Postcode ...........................................

**Send this whole page to:**
**UK: FREEPOST CN81, Croydon, CR9 3WZ**
**EIRE: PO Box 4546, Kilcock, County Kildare (stamp required)**

Offer valid in UK and Eire only and not available to current Reader Service subscribers to this series. We reserve the right to refu: an application and applicants must be aged 18 years or over. Only one application per household. Terms and prices subject change without notice. Offer expires 31st December 2001. As a result of this application, you may receive further offers fr: Harlequin Mills & Boon Limited and other carefully selected companies. If you would prefer not to share in this opportunity ple: write to The Data Manager at the address above.

Silhouette® is a registered trademark used under license.
Sensation™ is being used as a trademark.